The Broken Blade

◆

The
Broken Blade

◆

William Durbin

DELACORTE PRESS

I would like to extend special thanks to my editors, Kathleen Squires and Timothy Robinson, for their insightful suggestions; and to my agent, Barbara Markowitz, for believing in both me and the beauty of the canoe country.

I am also grateful to the staff of the Hibbing Public Library and the Minnesota Historical Society for their help with my research, and to the special people who went out of their way to encourage me, including Jessica, Reid, Gregory, Honoré, John, and the HAT class at Washington Elementary in Hibbing, Minnesota.

Published by
Delacorte Press
Bantam Doubleday Dell Publishing Group, Inc.
1540 Broadway
New York, New York 10036

Copyright © 1997 by William C. Durbin

Library of Congress Cataloging-in-Publication Data
Durbin, William C.
  The broken blade / William Durbin.
    p. cm.
  Summary: When an injury prevents his father from going into northern Canada with fur traders, thirteen-year-old Pierre decides to take his father's place as a *voyageur*.
  ISBN 0-385-32224-0 (alk. paper)
  [1. Fur traders—Fiction.   2. Canada—History—1763–1867—Fiction.   3. Fathers and sons—Fiction.]   I. Title.
PZ7.D9323Br   1997
[Fic]—dc20   96-22114
                                                        CIP
                                                         AC

The text of this book is set in 12-point Century Old Style.

Book design by Trish Parcell Watts
Manufactured in the United States of America

March 1997

10   9   8   7   6   5   4   3   2

To Barbara,
with love

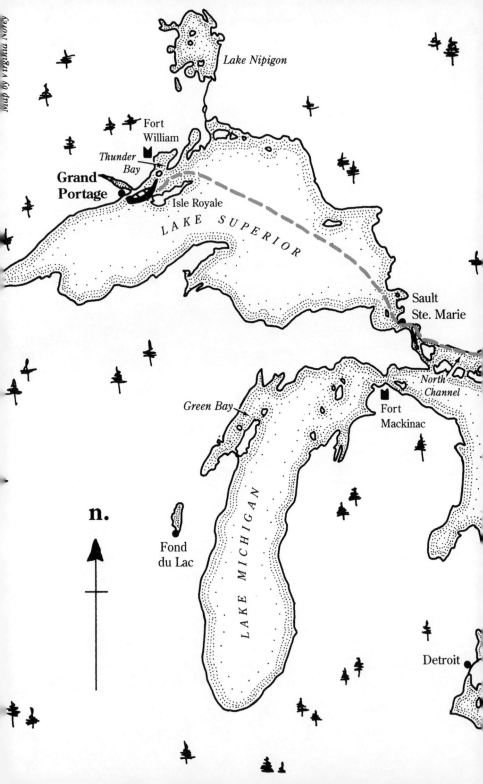

Lake Nipigon

Fort William

Thunder Bay

Grand Portage

Isle Royale

L A K E   S U P E R I O R

Sault Ste. Marie

North Channel

Green Bay

Fort Mackinac

n.

Fond du Lac

L A K E   M I C H I G A N

Detroit

Pierre's Journey
1800

Scale of Miles

| 0 | 50 | 100 | 150 | 200 |

Lake Nipissing

Trout Lake

French River

Montréal

Lachin

Georgian Bay

Ottawa River

St. Lawrence River

LAKE HURON

Nottawasaga Bay

Barrie

Toronto

LAKE ONTARIO

Oswego

Niagara Falls

Albany

Buffalo

LAKE ERIE

Erie

Cleveland

Author's Note

Furs were a symbol of status and power in medieval Europe. Strict laws dictated that only royalty could wear ermine, sable, and marten. Less valuable furs such as beaver and mink were worn by the middle class, while poor people were limited to rabbit, lamb, and sometimes cat.

As the middle class grew, so did the demand for furs. Convinced that North America contained a wealth of fur-bearing animals, French explorers of the seventeenth century such as Father Nicolet, Sieur des Groseilliers, and Pierre Radisson laid claim to vast tracts of land that became known as New France.

With the cooperation of dozens of Native American tribes who agreed to exchange pelts for trade goods, Pierre La Vérendrye, Sir Alexander Mackenzie, David Thompson, Alexander Henry, and other later adventurers mapped out canoe routes and established posts along the frontier. Thus began the era of the *voyageur.*

From the 1700s on, these French-Canadian canoemen were hired to transport trade goods and furs over the four-thousand-mile waterway that extended from Montréal to the Pacific Ocean. Paddling sixteen to eighteen hours a day and portaging 180-pound loads, *voyageurs* were legendary for their endurance and good humor. They lived hard and in many cases died young, but their irrepressible and adventuresome spirit still serves as a perfect model for modern-day canoeists who paddle through the Quetico-Superior wilderness and dream of the north country beyond.

William Durbin
LAKE VERMILION, MINNESOTA, June 1996

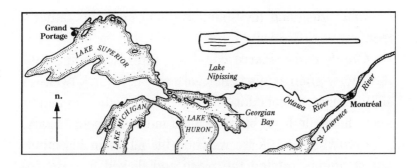

CHAPTER 1

◆

An Errant Stroke

PIERRE WOKE TO the sound of an ax. The thunk of the blade on the chopping block told him that his father was splitting dry pine. Now that it was spring, his mother let the fires die out during the warm part of the day. That meant she needed more kindling than she did during the winter.

At thirteen years of age Pierre knew he should be up and helping. It had been his job to keep the woodbox filled since he was ten, but it was Saturday, and it felt good to lie in bed a few extra minutes. Besides, the heavy work was done, and he knew his father enjoyed making kindling.

Chunk, crack. The ax snapped down. Pierre closed his

eyes and imagined the splinters piling up at his father's feet.

Chunk, crack. Pierre could see the blade biting into the knotty grain as his father gave the ax a quick twist—a splitting lick, he called it—to shave the wood clean and to keep the blade from burying itself in the chopping block.

Chunk, crack. Pierre watched his father in his mind. Quick fingers rotated the piece and flicked free the instant before the ax fell. *Chunk, crack, chunk* . . . Despite the sharp crackling of the pine shearing off, there was a rhythm to the sound that made Pierre drowsy.

He drifted back to sleep and dreamed of riding in an open carriage down a broad, cobbled street bathed in green-gold light. The air smelled of polished leather and coal smoke and dew. Ahead Pierre saw the River Seine and the towering Cathedral of Notre Dame. Beyond the bright music of the clattering hooves, a boatman sang. Pierre listened, but he couldn't understand the song. He tilted his head to better hear the strange words.

Just then the shadow of an enormous bird arched out over the river. There was a dark croaking sound, followed by a human cry. Pierre jerked his head back.

"Sweet Mother of God," the voice groaned. Pierre's eyes opened wide. For a moment he was lost between sleep and waking.

"Charles?" his mother called from the kitchen. "Are you all right?"

By the time Pierre pulled on his pants and ran out the

door, Mother was already outside. Father sat cross-legged on the ground beside the chopping block, cradling his left hand in his right. The dark hair at his temples glistened with sweat.

His mother bent to take one look and then stood up. Her cheeks were pale. "Camille," she called back into the house, to Pierre's older sister, "bring a towel. Quickly."

She turned to her son. "Get the doctor, Pierre. You must get the doctor." But Pierre stood openmouthed, staring at the bright blood that pumped from his father's half-severed thumb.

"Pierre!" Mother shouted, cuffing his shoulder. "Go, now. The doctor."

Pierre ran down the path toward the village of Lachine. As he sprinted down the trail, he thought of the blood at their annual fall slaughter. His head pounded with the ringing of the butcher's steel. He saw the blade flash and the blood and the fire-blackened kettle. He smelled the stubbly hides that hung, scraped and stinking, against the barn wall each November.

Reaching Dr. Guilliard's house, Pierre pounded on the heavy door. "Doctor," he gasped. "Dr. Guilliard."

When the door swung open, Pierre froze. It was Dr. Guilliard's daughter, Celeste. Her fine black hair hung loosely over a white shawl. Tall and graceful, Celeste was the prettiest girl in his class at school. She and Pierre had often played together when they were little. Hiking in the woods beyond Pierre's house, they'd picked flowers for their mothers and played hide-and-seek with friends. Sometimes they pushed each other on the swing that Pierre's father had tied to a huge oak tree behind the woodshed. If they pumped extra hard, they could swing high enough to glimpse a tall church spire in Montréal. But in the past few years Celeste had been too busy to spend time with Pierre or any of the other village boys. Every Saturday private tutors came to teach her piano and dance and other skills deemed by her mother to be appropriate for a young lady. Though she and Pierre were the same age, Celeste suddenly seemed older.

Pierre looked into her pale blue eyes and blushed. He lowered his head. "There's been an accident."

"Papa," Celeste called down the hallway.

Dr. Guilliard appeared, his breakfast napkin in hand. "What is it, son?"

"My father . . . cut bad . . . an ax . . ."

The doctor turned and reached for his frock coat and bag. "Settle down," he said, "everything will be all right."

Pierre tried to help the doctor saddle his horse, but Guilliard pushed him aside. He pulled the cinch cord tight, tied his bag to his saddle bow, and was off, the tails of his coat flying up behind. Long after the doctor was out of sight, Pierre could hear his instrument bag bouncing and rattling.

Starting up the trail at a jog, Pierre was suddenly angry with himself. The kindling was *his* job. He should have swung that ax. His own thumb should be chopped to a bloody stub.

He wondered how his family would survive if Father couldn't work. Each spring Father signed on as a *voyageur* for the North West Company, but Pierre knew that no canoe brigade would hire a crippled steersman.

The closer Pierre got to home, the more slowly he walked. He stopped at the edge of a clearing, just out of sight of his house, and looked across the greening valley. "Make him be all right," he whispered, half in prayer.

By the time Pierre reached home, Dr. Guilliard had finished dressing Father's wound and was talking with Mother in the kitchen. "I am sorry, *madame*," he said, "but when the bone is cut through there is so little we can do."

Pierre's heart went cold. Would his father die? He ran to the back bedroom. As he threw open the door, Camille jumped up from her bedside chair and waved at him to be quiet. Father groaned, "What's that?" and turned his head toward the door.

He was pale. His forehead was beaded with sweat, and his eyes were half open. The room smelled of blackberry brandy. "Eh, Pierre," he whispered, pausing to take in a shallow breath. "I'm glad you're back. You took so long."

Pierre resolved to be brave. But when he saw the bloodstained bandage on his father's hand, lying upon his father's chest, he started to cry, even though he knew it was the worst thing he could do.

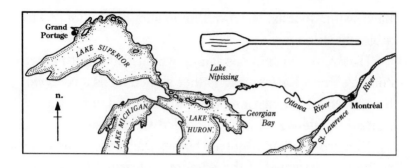

CHAPTER 2

Pierre's Plan

ON MONDAY MORNING Pierre visited with his father before he left for school. Pierre sat carefully down beside him.

"You know," Pierre said, "this wouldn't have happened if I'd been—"

Father interrupted him. "It's not your fault I chopped off my thumb," he said, scowling at the heavy bandage in disgust. Short, dark, and always energetic, Father was never one to hide his feelings. His voice resounded with conviction; the same voice that loved to sing and tell stories.

Pierre stared at the wrapped thumb, imagining the stub and its stitched flap of skin. What he wanted to say

6

was, *Tell the truth, Father. Tell how my laziness has crippled you.*

"You'll not hear this *hivernant* complain about anything but his own clumsiness," Pierre's father continued. "Why, I was wielding an ax when I was half your size."

"But if I'd—"

"I'll hear none of it. And I'll thank you to not manufacture excuses for me. I'm old enough to know the difference between a stick of wood and my thumb."

As Pierre left the bedroom, he heard the nervous whispers of his mother and his sister. He knew what they were talking about: His father was scheduled to sign his engagement papers with the North West Company this very week.

Like most of the men in Lachine, Canada, Pierre's father was a *voyageur* who freighted goods from Montréal to Grand Portage. He knew the Ottawa River system and the Great Lakes as well as any man alive, and the canoes he guided were famous for their speed.

If Father couldn't sign on, Camille, who was already seventeen, could work as a maid or housekeeper to help the family survive. They might manage if Mother could do the same, but she needed to take care of Pierre's baby sister, Claire.

When Pierre sat down to breakfast, Camille asked, "Are you all right?" He ignored her, hating the way she babied him lately. Since she'd got an engagement ring last Christmas from a Montréal boy, it was as if he had two mothers. She was always ordering him around, and to make matters worse, she had a loud voice like Father's. Even a casual comment sounded irritatingly bossy. Pierre couldn't wait until she married next summer and moved into a house of her own.

As he ate, Pierre watched little Claire tug at Camille's hair ribbon. Though Claire had spent the first six months of her life crying, she was smiling a lot lately. Last week she had even pointed at Pierre and said "Ba," a word he proudly insisted meant brother. If this baby had to go hungry because of him, Pierre would never forgive himself. But what could he do?

After breakfast, Pierre left for school. Pierre's mother insisted he go to school, even though most of his friends had left the schoolroom and gone to work. Like Father, Mother wasn't shy about her opinions. She'd always told her son that he would be a great man someday. She hoped he would become a judge, a merchant, or even a priest, but Pierre didn't care to look that far ahead.

School had always been easy for Pierre, but now that he was thirteen and the oldest boy still enrolled, he was bored. Sister Marguérite tried to make things more interesting by having him tutor the younger students, but tutoring was dull compared with the stories his working friends told of their lives as canoemen, lumberjacks, and apprentice tradesmen. He was tired of being a mere schoolboy when everyone else had entered the real world. They were driving wagons and piloting riverboats and voyaging in canoes while he was stuck memorizing Latin verbs.

This morning, though he told no one of his plan, he walked straight past his school to the waterfront district and the main depot of the North West Company. The riverbank was crowded with at least twelve dozen men. The *voyageurs* were dressed in red caps, short shirts tied with bright sashes, breechclouts, deerskin leggings, and moccasins. They were all busy packing trade goods or working on their canoes.

Pierre felt nervous and out of place. He'd never stayed away from school before, and he worried about what his mother would think. During breakfast, when he'd planned this trip in his mind, he'd thought it would be easy to find a company clerk or one of his father's friends, but he had no idea where to begin in this maze of men.

He walked over to a fellow who was holding a torch in one hand and dripping a ball of pitch onto the seams of a canoe. Pierre tapped the man on the shoulder, "Excuse me, sir, could—"

The man stood up and growled, "What you want with Bellegarde?"

Pierre quickly drew back. This was the ugliest man he'd ever seen. The man's hair was thin and scraggly; one of his earlobes was missing; and the left side of his face was pushed toward the center. White scars ran along his cheek and nose in stark relief against his dark face.

"I was looking . . . I mean, could you tell me . . ."

The fumes from the torch burned Pierre's eyes. He coughed.

The *voyageur* threw back his head and laughed. One front tooth was missing. "You used to prettier men than André Bellegarde," he said. "But I tell you, I'm best-looking fellow you'll ever see who wrestled a grizzly bear and lost. One swipe to the head"—he pointed to the jagged scars with the warm pitch block in his hand—"is all it took to make this mess."

"I . . ." Pierre could think of nothing to say. "I'm sorry."

"Save your pity for the dead, boy." Bellegarde spat into the sand at Pierre's feet. "Besides, that bear's worse off than me." He rattled the bear-claw necklace that hung down the front of his leather shirt. "Don't never be sorry for no man what's still alive."

Pierre stared at the bear claws, as huge as a man's fingers, and his eyes widened. "Please. I'm looking for your brigade chief."

"McKay," the man said, pointing with his torch toward a log storehouse just up the riverbank.

For a moment Pierre thought about heading back to the schoolhouse. He liked to go slowly, to consider every option, but he could tell that these men plunged headlong into their work. As he walked cautiously up the bank, men hurried by on all sides, carrying bundles of trade goods and laughing and whistling. One man with a powder keg on each shoulder called out, "Step aside, boy, these casks got more bite than you'd care to handle."

This was the company his father kept. Dark-skinned, with heavily muscled arms and shoulders, each man carried two ninety-pound bales of cargo on his back. A few swaggering fellows hauled three parcels without complaint.

As Pierre studied the men, he recalled the first time his father brought him down to this landing. He was only seven or eight. One of the last brigades of the season was just arriving, and Father hoisted him on his shoulders so he could see over the gathering crowd. Pierre counted twenty-four canoes.

"It's the biggest brigade of the year," Father said. Then he whispered, "There's more than a million dollars' worth of pelts in those canoes. Not bad for a single season of fur trade with the Indians, eh?"

"A million dollars?" Pierre repeated.

"Yes." Father nodded. "And the lot of it paddled and portaged more than a thousand miles from Grand Portage, just so gentlemen can wear beaver-pelt hats."

"Hats?" Pierre looked at his father's simple red cap.

"Beaver hats this tall," Father said, raising his hand to an absurd height above his head, "for fancy gents to wear when they walk with fancy ladies."

When Pierre reached the top of the riverbank, there was no mistaking Commander McKay. He stood half a head taller than any of the men clustered around him. Bushy red hair covered his face and ringed his balding head, and he was dressed more like a banker than a frontiersman. An unlit briar pipe stuck out of his vest pocket; a pencil stub was tucked behind one ear. He was deep in conversation with another man.

When McKay finally noticed Pierre, he stopped. "What'll it be, laddie?"

"I've come to engage, sir," Pierre said.

"Bit young, aren't ye?"

Pierre lied, "I'm nearly fourteen." He had just turned thirteen the month before. But at five feet, five inches and 130 pounds, he was confident he could do the work of a man, though he knew his boyish face and cropped hair made him look young.

"Sorry, but we don't have time to play nursemaid. Our trips are a hard push all the way." McKay looked again at his list.

Pierre's face reddened as he struggled to think of a reply. He knew McKay wouldn't care that he could spell well or that he'd won Sister's geography prize three years in a row. He hated himself for his shyness. Why couldn't he be loud and bold like his father?

Finally he said, "I can paddle hard. I really can. My father, Charles La Page, has worked for the North West since he was twelve."

"That's all well and good," McKay replied without

looking up, "but it's steersmen we need, lad. We've middlemen enough to paddle us clear to China."

Pierre thought of little Claire and the hard winter his family would face without Father's wages. He had to think of something. But before he could speak again, a voice spoke up. "Pardon me, Mr. McKay." A thin, light-skinned man with gray eyes strolled up to Pierre. "Did you say you were Charles La Page's son?"

"Yes, I am."

Stepping closer to Pierre, the man stopped and stared. Suddenly he made a fist and touched it to the tip of Pierre's chin. His rock-hard knuckles tilted Pierre's head back.

The fellow grinned and clapped Pierre on the shoulder, nearly knocking him over. "That blond hair could've fooled me, but you got Charlie's firm jaw—square-like, with that little hollow. Can you take a punch like your pa?" The man held up his fist again and grinned.

McKay looked up. "You and this La Page fellow mates, Charbonneau?"

"We wintered together up in Athabasca. If he's Charlie's son I'll vouch for him."

"You sure?"

"I could use one more middleman in my canoe."

"That's fine with me, but you see it through."

"Yes, sir." Charbonneau touched his cap. "I will, sir."

Though Pierre was grateful to Charbonneau for helping, the man's pushy, military manner made Pierre nervous. Pierre's father made fun of soldiers—he called them "silly saluters who love to play dress-up"—and Charbonneau seemed to be that type.

Without another word, McKay drew out an official-looking piece of parchment. He lifted the glass stopper from his inkwell and dipped in his goose-quill pen. Writing in bold script, McKay filled in Pierre's engagement papers with the date—May 11, 1800—and his full name.

McKay then handed the pen to Pierre. When Pierre signed his name to the contract and didn't just make an X like most of the men, McKay said, "What do you think of that, Charbonneau? Any lad who writes such a strong hand should be a fine paddler."

Charbonneau made no comment. He frowned at the fancy writing on the contract.

Next, while McKay checked each item off on a list, Charbonneau issued Pierre the standard North West Company supplies: a blanket, a shirt, a pair of trousers, two handkerchiefs, and a two-pound twist of carrot tobacco. When Charbonneau counted out the one-third advance on a year's salary, Pierre felt proud, knowing he'd done the right thing.

McKay then concluded Pierre's engagement by shaking his hand and saying, "Just make sure you stay clear of those Hudson's Bay rascals."

Knowing how much the North West men hated their

archrival, the Hudson's Bay Company, Pierre quickly said, "I will, sir."

McKay then turned to Charbonneau. "Have him work with La Petite today. That should keep him busy."

Charbonneau nodded with a wry smile and marched around the table toward a log storehouse. Charbonneau was long-legged and lean compared to the other *voyageurs*. His quick movements reminded Pierre of Monsieur Marolt, a man who owned a combined livery stable and funeral parlor in Lachine. Charbonneau had the same sort of thin face, all sharp points and angles.

Pierre had to walk fast to keep up. He wondered what sort of a fellow this little La Petite might be. Just before they passed through the low doorway of the storehouse, McKay called after them, "Make sure La Petite has secured that last Montréal canoe."

Charbonneau turned and acknowledged McKay's command. "Aye, sir."

"And tell him to make sure she's caulked tight. The last we hired from that scoundrel Langlois leaked like a rotten thatch job."

With one last "Aye," Charbonneau led Pierre into the storeroom. The only light inside was cast by an oil lamp. Pierre had never seen such vast piles of goods. Bolts of calico cloth and ribbon, and crates crammed with bells and colored beads and mirrors and sewing materials, were piled on shelves that lined either wall. Stacked around the room were other boxes that held spears, ice chisels, and gaff hooks for trapping beaver during the winter. Kegs and nested copper kettles were stacked near the entry. The thought of hauling all these trade goods the length of the Great Lakes suddenly made Pierre uneasy. Anyone can sign his name and pocket his salary, he thought, but what about portaging cooking pots and musket balls and thirty-five-foot lake canoes?

"La Petite?" Charbonneau called, squinting into the half dark. "Where's that fellow gone now?" he mumbled.

"La Petite?" Charbonneau tried again, stepping forward and calling twice as loudly. Out of the corner of his eye, Pierre thought he saw a dim shadow, but before he could turn, two hands seized his ankles from behind and suddenly jerked his feet out from under him.

"*Eeee . . .*" Pierre threw out his hands to keep his face from smashing into the dirt floor. An instant later he was swinging upside down, staring at the largest pair of moccasins he had ever seen.

"Let me go!" Pierre yelled.

Someone laughed uproariously. "So what have you brought me, Charbonneau? Something to shelve or to stick in a nice little keg?"

Charbonneau laughed as La Petite swung Pierre up toward the rafters and let go of his ankles. Pierre squealed again, thinking for a moment that this giant intended to kill him. But La Petite caught the boy by his armpits just as he began to fall and set him back down.

"That's a good one, La Petite," Charbonneau chortled.

"Hiding in the dark. You do know how to spook a fellow. Meet your helper for the day, Pierre La Page."

This fellow they called La Petite was the biggest and the blackest Frenchman Pierre had ever seen. His frizzy black hair brushed the log tie beams overhead. His pants and shirt were deerskin and smelled as if they'd been tanned with pig brains and smoke.

When La Petite reached out his hand, Pierre took a step back and trampled Charbonneau's foot. "Stand still, boy," Charbonneau ordered, pushing him forward again. Pierre braced himself, afraid to imagine what this giant would do to him next.

"Please pardon my behavior, *monsieur,*" La Petite said, bowing at the waist and pretending to remove a cap from his bare head, "had I known you were my assistant, I would not have treated you so rudely." He then let out a deep chuckle and tousled Pierre's hair.

"To work now," he added, and started toward the rear of the building, expecting Pierre to follow.

And Pierre did follow, all morning and all afternoon without stopping. Accustomed to the calm of school, Pierre was amazed at the frantic pace La Petite maintained. They sorted trade goods. They hauled supplies to another warehouse on a big flatbed wagon. They inspected the new Montréal canoe at the boat works.

Pierre learned a lot about fur trade merchandise, and he was glad to discover that the giant La Petite was a gentle and fair fellow. La Petite explained each job to

Pierre and was patient with Pierre's questions. Unlike the intense Charbonneau, he walked with a relaxed stride, whistling or humming as he worked.

The big man even took Pierre's side late that afternoon when an evil-looking character confronted Pierre just after they'd returned from the boat works. "Who's your little lady friend, La Petite?" the man said, sneering at Pierre with the black, unblinking eyes of a snake.

"Leave my grandpa alone, Beloît," La Petite said, wagging a finger in his face. "He's a good worker."

Unafraid of La Petite's warning, Beloît spat in the dust at Pierre's feet and said, "Send him to the dressmaker."

Pierre couldn't help staring at Beloît. He wore a soiled shirt, open at the neck, and his chest was covered with matted black hair. His ragged beard and stooped shoulders made him look more like a bear than a man. But the thing that startled Pierre most was his nose—the right half had been ripped off.

Beloît scowled one last time and walked away grumbling to himself. As soon as he was out of earshot, Pierre asked La Petite, "What happened to him?"

"That's quite a nose, ain't it?" La Petite chuckled. "Why, he's a fighter, Grandpa. He just loves to scrap. One day a fellow with very big teeth bit the starboard side of his nose clean off." La Petite grinned at the shock on Pierre's face.

"I'm meeting all the pretty ones today, aren't I?" Pierre said good-naturedly.

"That you are." La Petite clapped him on the back and turned to board his wagon.

So now Pierre had a nickname. These *voyageurs,* who loved to call the tallest man in their brigade by the French word for Shorty would name a smooth-faced boy such as him Grandpa.

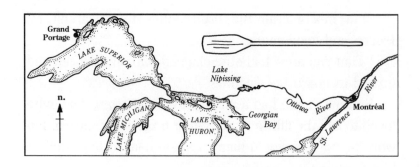

CHAPTER 3

Adieu

PIERRE WAS IN no hurry to get home. All his life he'd been a thinker, not a doer, a boy who considered every possibility before making a decision. Today was the first time he'd ever done anything this impulsive. Now he was scared. If only he'd talked it over with his parents. He knew his father would be proud of his enrolling, but he was afraid even to think of facing his mother.

Pierre paused by the company storehouse to look downriver. The lonely laughter of a loon echoed across the dark water. The loons traveled north and would be leaving, like him, any day now. And leaving with Pierre would be a lifetime of his mother's dreams.

On the way home Pierre passed Dr. Guilliard's house and hung his head. He was still ashamed at how he had handled the accident.

It was nearly dark by the time Pierre arrived at his cabin. When Pierre finally opened the cabin door, he spotted his parents sitting at the kitchen table having tea. Except for the bandaged hand that he rested on the table, Father looked strong.

"You're home at last." Mother rose to greet Pierre but stopped when she saw the paper and the long twist of tobacco in his hands. Every spring Father marched proudly through the door with these same articles. Every long summer Mother waited for his brigade to return home.

She stood stock-still, pressing one finger to her temple as she stared at her son. She didn't say anything, but her eyes showed disappointment.

Pierre placed his engagement papers and tobacco ration on the plank table. Father stared at the document before him. He slowly began to grin. "You've signed on?" He rose from the table and embraced Pierre. "My son the *voyageur*!" he said proudly.

When Pierre pulled out his salary advance and presented it to his mother, tears welled up in her eyes. "No," she protested, "you must keep some for yourself."

Pierre only shook his head, knowing if he tried to speak he would cry too.

*   *   *

Later that evening, while they sat before the fire, Pierre's father asked his son about the men he'd met. He praised Charbonneau and La Petite as fair and dependable, frowning only when he heard the name of Beloît, the fellow who'd teased Pierre. "Jean Beloît is a scoundrel," Father said, "though as good a bowman as you'll find."

"But no matter who you're paired with," Father added, "be sure to pull your own weight, and most important of all, don't complain. There's no place for laggers or whiners among canoemen. Never forget, either, that patience is your best friend in the North. You'll save many a carry by thinking your course through to the end. To the *voyageur,* the route is everything."

Father paused then and pulled deeply on his little clay pipe. Pierre listened carefully.

"I want you to know it is a good life if you make it so. When I was your age I met a man at the fort in Sault Sainte Marie who claimed fifty years of service to the Hudson's Bay Company. One evening he said to me, 'Charles, my whole life has been the canoes. Every river, every portage, every wife and song and sled dog that I knew was a pleasure, perfect in itself. Were all my days given back to me, I would make no other choice than to be a *voyageur.*'"

Pierre nodded, firm in his decision and ready for the adventure.

* * *

Long after Pierre had gone to bed, his mind whirled with pictures of the day: the giant, La Petite; the laughing faces of Charbonneau and Bellegarde; the evil sneer of Jean Beloît.

When sleep came, Pierre dreamed he was paddling alone up a narrow, rocky river. The current was so swift he used all his strength to keep the canoe from being swept downstream. He pulled hard until he came around a sharp bend. There, along the bank as far as he could see, stood his classmates from school. Sister Marguérite's voice was in the background, saying, "A true gift for learning is rare, my boy. Think what you could have become—a scholar, a lawyer, a . . ."

Just then there was a thunderous roar. A wall of water hit the bow, catapulting him into the river.

"Ahhhhhh . . . ," Pierre yelled as the water swept over him, pushing him down, down. His body cartwheeled in the blackness. The icy water churned over him as he struggled to find a footing on the slippery rocks.

When Pierre woke up, he was tangled in his blankets, and his heart was hammering in his throat.

A moment later, the leather-hinged door of his parents' bedroom creaked. Pierre lay still.

Mother whispered, "Are you all right?"

He coughed. "I'm fine."

"Are you sure?" She stepped forward to touch his forehead. "I thought I heard something."

"I'm all right." He fought to calm himself. His heart still pounded hard from his nightmare.

Pierre lay awake for a long time after Mother left. Out his bedroom window, upstream, the sky was a wilderness of stars. He was floating in blue-black light, lost in the depths of a dark river. Pierre tried to think of gentler things, but he was haunted by his dream. And every time he closed his eyes, he felt as if he were lying at the bottom of a watery grave.

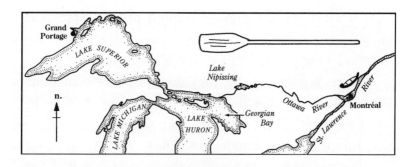

CHAPTER 4

Departure

ON WEDNESDAY PIERRE stopped by the school to say good-bye. It was recess, and he was the center of attention.

"Whose brigade are you in?"

"When do you leave?"

"How many miles will you paddle?"

As Pierre answered the questions, his eyes searched the schoolyard for Celeste Guilliard.

When Pierre finally saw her, standing at the rear entrance with her friends, recess was nearly over. As he stepped away from the boys, Celeste waved.

By the time Pierre crossed the school yard and reached her side, Sister Marguérite was ringing the bell.

Celeste's two friends giggled a moment, then left them alone.

"So I hear you're headed north," she said.

Pierre wanted to say something clever—something she would remember during the long summer while he was gone—but all he could manage was "Yes."

"Isn't that an awfully long paddle?"

"It's twenty-four hundred miles," Pierre replied. He wanted to say more. But the yard was nearly empty, and she was turning to leave. Pierre the thinker, Pierre the bookworm, was mumbling away his last chance.

"You know how Sister is about tardiness," Celeste said as she started up the steps.

This was his last chance. Pierre reached out to touch her hand, and when she turned, he decided to risk it. If he had the courage to sign up for a two-thousand-mile canoe trip, he should have the nerve to kiss a pretty girl.

His aim wasn't perfect, but he managed to graze her lips. Then, to his surprise, she gave him a quick kiss in return.

Celeste's eyes were bright, and her cheeks were flushed as she ran up the steps, calling out one last "Goodbye." For a moment Pierre stood alone in the empty yard, almost wishing he could step back into the comfortable world of readings and recitations.

"Be good," Mother said as she leaned forward and gave her son a quick peck on the cheek. Pierre nodded and took one last look at his little sister, who was nestled in Camille's arms half asleep. "You take care of your sister," Pierre whispered, tickling Claire's chin until she smiled.

Then Pierre turned to shake his father's hand one last time. Without thinking, Father clapped Pierre on the back with his injured hand and cursed at the sudden pain.

Pierre looked concerned, but Father laughed and waved his bandage toward Mother. "Don't worry. Your mother will take care of me. You watch your backside and keep your powder dry."

Up and down the shore of the St. Lawrence, families gathered as all five Montréal canoes were checked one last time. Pierre was sorry La Petite wasn't one of his fourteen canoe mates, but his father's old friend Charbonneau was the steersman, and a grinning, white-haired man they called La Londe manned the bow. Pierre recognized one of his fellow middlemen, a young man named Emile Duval who had left school only last year. Pierre was glad to see the scarred man, Bellegarde, walk toward another canoe.

The *voyageurs* paraded in their finest breechclouts, shirts, and sashes. They all wore new moccasins and elegantly plumed red caps. The forty-foot canoes were moored in the shallows, already loaded with a winter's worth of trade goods. The gunwales of each birch bark craft were painted with bright stripes, and NORTH WEST COMPANY decorated each bow. Flags hung from the stern poles, and vermilion-tipped paddles stood propped in each craft.

McKay, dressed in buckskin like an ordinary crewman, nodded to Charbonneau, and the boarding began.

As Beloît stepped past McKay, he pointed to Pierre and said, "If that puppy is coming with us, I hope you checked to see that he's housebroken."

A few men chuckled as Beloît cackled and slapped his thigh.

Pierre's ears burned. He hoped his father hadn't heard. He waded into the icy water up to his knees and stepped carefully into the canoe he would be paddling for the next twelve weeks.

He knew from his father how fragile these Montréal canoes were. Though they carried two and a half tons of freight, their birch bark skin demanded care in boarding and required the men to sit still as they paddled. Too much shifting of weight strained the laced-root and gummed construction. Once the trade goods were delivered to the fort in Grand Portage, the company sometimes purchased new canoes to carry their valuable cargo of furs home at summer's end.

The other night Father explained, "Rough handling means days lost in repairs, and lost days is lost dollars to the North West."

Pierre took his place among the twelve middlemen in his canoe. Someone on the bank fired a pistol, and the crowd cheered. As the men around him shouted farewells, Pierre waved his cap toward his family and called, "Goodbye." His stomach sank at how final that word sounded this morning.

Charbonneau pushed the stern of Pierre's canoe clear of the shallows. "To the North," he called, and the bowman La Londe let out a whistle from his post and waved his paddle overhead.

Without another word, the men suddenly dipped their paddles in unison. Struggling to catch up, Pierre grabbed his blade and pulled hard.

There was a whirl of color as five dozen paddles turned the river to froth. As the canoes started up the river, Pierre's dog, Pepper, and a few other dogs ran along the shore, barking. Every year these first miles proved who had the fastest canoe, and as long as they were within sight of shore, the men would pull for all they were worth.

Charbonneau's canoe held its position in the middle of the brigade until they were a quarter of a mile out. Then the fourth canoe crept past. Pierre tried to keep up with the windmilling blades around him. He prayed they could hold off the last canoe until they rounded the southern tip of Lachine and passed from the crowd's view. Pierre knew his father was watching from shore. Each spring Father studied the first brigades to depart. He always scorned the last canoe out as "a sad excuse for canoemen."

La Petite was chanting an old French song from the

stern of the trailing craft. "Row brothers, row," he sang. "The river runs fast. The daylight fades fast . . ." Pierre knew that good singers were prized as *voyageurs*. A lively little middleman named Michel Larocque helped the bowman, La Londe, lead the same chant in Pierre's canoe.

"Put your backs into it," Charbonneau commanded.

"Give it all you've got, fellows," La Londe sang out, in a voice rich and loud like Pierre's father's.

Pierre paddled as hard as he could. He knew they would blame him, as the youngest member of the crew, if they fell behind. Studying Emile, who was sitting right in front of him, Pierre leaned forward with each stroke and jerked back hard, trying to match his pace.

They kept up until Charbonneau turned his canoe around the southernmost point of Lachine. There La Petite cut between them and the shore. As he glided past, he called, "Paddle, Grandpa. Paddle," and laughed. "You'll not get home before the frost if you drag your blade that slow."

The men in both canoes joined in the fun. "Grandpa?" Charbonneau echoed. "That's a good one."

Pierre's face, flushed from exertion, reddened even more. He swallowed his anger and pulled fierce and deep on his paddle.

An hour later, the canoes had settled down to a moderate pace, but Pierre's arms were aching, his back was sore, and his hair was plastered to his temples with sweat.

How could he ever paddle twenty-four hundred miles? His father warned him, too, that poor weather could extend the twelve-week trip by a month or more.

To break the monotony he counted his strokes. One, two, three . . . he silently marked each pull. At first it took his mind off the pain, but by the time he got to five hundred, he knew he'd made a mistake. Pierre glanced over his shoulder, amazed at how slowly they were moving. He could run that far in five minutes.

To cheer the men on, La Londe and Michel Larocque started up another song, but Pierre didn't listen. He counted instead. When he got to his thousandth stroke he refused to look back. By the time he reached two thousand, he realized it was taking as much effort to count as it was to paddle, but he kept at it just the same. Just to prove that he could, he would count this day through to the end.

Pierre thought back to school, recalling how he could balance a quill pen on the back of one finger and feel no weight. Right now he would trade places with anyone in his classroom. Pierre was a boy who liked to curl up with a book and ponder and dream, but he could already see there would be no time for dreaming in this life.

Lift. Pull. Lift. Pull. Twenty-five, twenty-six, twenty . . . His paddle felt like iron. As Pierre labored, he recalled a poem that Sister had him memorize last month. Telling the story of a hero called Aeneas who was cursed by the gods, the poem began:

Arms, and the man I sing, who, forced by fate
And haughty Juno's unrelenting hate
Expelled and exiled, left the Trojan shore
Long labors both by sea and land he bore.

When Pierre thought about the many years Aeneas wandered after the Trojan War, he was ashamed to be exhausted after only a single morning of paddling.

"*Demi-chargé!*" the steersman yelled.

Pierre looked up. They were at the base of a short rapids and had to paddle double-time against the current. "I said, '*Demi-chargé,*'" Charbonneau shouted, tipping Pierre's cap off with his long setting pole. The men laughed as Pierre ducked to grab his cap.

Though the current was swift, it was no match for their paddles. The moss-crowned rocks blurred beneath the white hull as Charbonneau chanted in military cadence: "Pull, pull, pull . . ." Out of the corner of his eye Pierre saw the muscles stand out on Charbonneau's forearms as he planted his setting pole and pushed hard.

At the top of the short cascade La Londe shouted, "Hard now!" and pulled double-time with his paddle. The bow rose and then fell as the canoe cut through the white funnel at the head of the rapids and glided into a still pool.

"Well done, gentlemen," said La Londe. Five dozen middlemen cheered and waved their paddles. Pierre knew if a canoe could be paddled up a rapids or pulled up with tracking ropes, the crew had reason to celebrate.

There was no harder job than portaging their ninety-pound bales around the places in the river that were too dangerous to paddle. Smart *voyageurs* would gladly paddle five miles out of their way to avoid even a half-mile carry.

At the head of the pool stood the little stone church of St. Anne, the patron saint of the *voyageurs*. Pierre's father often spoke of this place. Here North West traders and explorers paused to ask a blessing for their journeys.

Suddenly the cheering crewmen went silent. Still gasping for breath from his hard paddling, Pierre looked up to see the men in the lead canoe take their caps off all at once. A lone canoe approached the landing below the church, carrying a wooden coffin.

Emile asked Charbonneau, "Is that Bourgone?"

Charbonneau nodded. "One more cross for the Calumet." Pierre had heard of the famous crosses that marked the graves of *voyageurs* who died en route. "His name was Amble Bourgone," Charbonneau continued. "He drowned in the upper Ottawa just before freeze-up. His crewmen just dug his body out of its winter grave."

Though the day was warm, Pierre shivered at the thought of a body lying frozen beneath the snow. He imagined foxes and wolves pawing at the piled stones of the cairn, and mice seeking shelter in the corpse's pockets.

After the canoe and coffin passed, the men stopped by the church of St. Anne to make an offering. Pierre's arms ached as he stepped ashore. One by one they deposited their coins in the box at the front of the chapel and stepped inside to cross themselves and whisper a prayer. Even Mr. McKay dropped some money into the box.

Later the men lit clay pipes and sat quietly at the river's edge. A few walked off to be alone. This place marked the official beginning of their journey, yet no one looked north. Pierre stared at the dark green hills that lay upriver, wondering what they held.

When he finally turned his eyes toward home, his throat went tight. Father should be here, not me, he thought.

He closed his eyes and saw the flash of the blade and the blood. He saw the doctor reach for his black thread and bright needle. A hundred times he'd played the scene over in his mind, and it was always the same. He felt shame in his laziness and shame in knowing he wasn't brave enough to wish the stroke had fallen on his own hand instead.

"You ready to go?"

It was Emile Duval, his old schoolmate. Pierre nodded and stood up. Though Emile was two years older than Pierre, he'd been in the same grade. A tough farm boy, Emile wasn't stupid, but he often got behind by missing school during the planting and harvest seasons. Emile was known for his curly black hair, and he had a nervous habit of brushing his bangs away from his eyes.

As they walked to the waiting canoes, Emile grinned.

"Paddling sure beats reciting those Latin poems of Sister's, don't it?"

Pierre smiled weakly, thinking just the opposite. Unless the paddling got a whole lot easier, he'd prefer Latin any day.

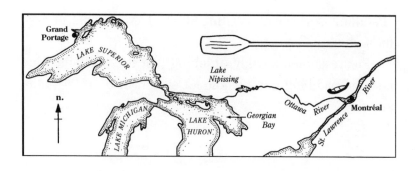

CHAPTER 5

◆

Massacre Island

BY LATE AFTERNOON the brigade reached the wide place in the Ottawa River called the Lake of Two Mountains. Pierre's hands were puffy and blistered from paddling. His arms and shoulders ached, and his shirt was soaked with sweat.

Charbonneau commanded, "Ship oars," and Pierre and the crewmen rested their paddles on the gunwales.

"That's only twenty-five miles today, fellows," the steersman said, "but we make up for our holiday tomorrow on the Long Sault."

Pierre wanted to ask Charbonneau if he was joking about today being a holiday, but he feared Charbonneau was serious.

Just then, McKay and La Petite pulled alongside.

"So which camp will it be, sir?" La Petite asked.

"We usually take the north," McKay replied.

"It's the north shore then," Charbonneau agreed, adding, "How about a little race to see who tends the fires tonight?"

La Petite looked toward Pierre. "Are you sure you're up to it with that crew of babies?"

A shout rose above the other voices. "Last canoe to shore gathers the wood!"

Yells went up from the other crewmen, and in an instant the water was churning with the force of seventy paddle blades. Amazed at the sudden energy, Pierre did what he could.

It was less than a half mile to the campsite, but that was too far for Pierre. Once he slipped on his forward stroke and splashed Emile. Another time his paddle twisted sideways. Charbonneau yelled, "Pull, La Page. Pull!" His voice was a whiplash.

Pierre glanced over his shoulder for help. Charbonneau nodded urgently at his own paddle and made a smooth stroke in the water, but Pierre's tired muscles managed only a weak chop.

By now the blisters on his right hand were bleeding.

When the last canoe in the brigade passed them, Charbonneau said, "Another day, men," and they slowed to their normal pace. No one was in a hurry to reach shore with teasing so sure to come.

Can one bad paddler in twelve mean that much? Pierre wondered. If he didn't improve, he knew he would be a burden to the whole crew. He remembered his father's advice: "Pull your own weight and you'll find no better friends than your canoe mates."

La Petite was waiting on the beach. "Glad to see you made it, fellows," he called. "I thought maybe you got lost and we needed to put together a search party." The crewmen laughed. Pierre hunched down and tried not to be noticed.

Even the quiet one, Bellegarde, joined in. "Eh, ladies," he called out as they unloaded, "you need some help maybe with those heavy parcels? Ha, Ha. It was a big day shopping, no?"

The catcalls continued as they carried the freight up the bank. After they finished, Charbonneau asked Pierre, "How's my middleman?" Though Charbonneau's voice was kind, his eyes were the cold gray of a soldier on a mission. Pierre could tell he hated weakness.

"Fine, sir," Pierre said, hiding the crusted blood on his palm.

But La Londe was right behind them. He took hold of Pierre's hand and turned it over. "It's the right one, eh? The hand closest to the water always takes a beating. The water softens the skin."

"It's all right." Pierre closed his hand as tightly as he could.

"Just the same," Charbonneau said, "we'll keep you on

the port side tomorrow. The sore one should dry out then."

La Londe agreed. "That should help. My hands were plenty soft when I was your age." Pierre couldn't imagine the broad-shouldered bowman ever having anything but callused hands, but he appreciated La Londe's gentle and fatherly tone. Pierre prayed that their plan would work. He worried that another day of paddling would turn his palm into mincemeat.

Gathering firewood was not as bad as Pierre expected. It felt good to work the kinks out of his legs, and he tried to carry more than his share of the wood.

As he bent to collect some kindling, Pierre felt the pain in his bottom for the first time. He wondered if the thin slats of the canoe seats could leave permanent creases on his backside.

Emile Duval approached him. "If you feel a little stiff, that's normal," Emile said, brushing a shock of hair out of his eyes.

"How long does it last?" Pierre asked. He was grateful for Emile's concern, and he knew that Emile would tell him the truth.

"In a couple of weeks you'll feel like you've been canoeing your whole life," Emile assured him. "Besides"—he grinned—"paddling is nothing compared to a day with Naggy Maggie."

Pierre smiled, recalling the nickname the older boys called Sister Marguérite. Pierre had to admit that Sister could be mean at times, especially to the poorer students. "How nice of you to grace us with your presence, Monsieur Duval," she would greet Emile when he returned to school after a week of work in the fields.

Emile meant to comfort Pierre, but two weeks sounded like forever. Since Emile was used to plowing and grubbing stumps and pitching hay, paddling was like a vacation for him. But the small chores Pierre had done around his cabin left him unprepared for this brutal work. To make matters worse, he worried that his years of schooling might have made him too soft to endure the voyage. What if his studies had turned him into a pale coward—a creature too frail to do anything but turn the pages in a book? Though he hated to admit it, Pierre knew he would rather do a month of algebra lessons than repeat the day of labor that had bloodied his hands.

The evening meal was lye-soaked corn boiled with a few ounces of salt pork. It didn't appeal to Pierre, but the crewmen quickly lined up at the ten-gallon kettle, took their portions on tin plates, and shoveled it down. They sat anywhere—on a log or a rock or the bare ground. Some didn't even bother with sitting.

They used homemade wooden spoons or just their hands, tipping their plates and licking up the last few morsels. Beloît remembered his spoon but could find no plate. Not caring to borrow a tin, he ate his meal out of his sweat-stained cap. As he sucked his fingers clean, Pierre looked away to keep from vomiting.

After dinner the men took their leisure with their pipes. Sitting before the fire and drawing out their tobacco pouches with great ceremony, they packed their clay bowls tight and then lit them with tapers pulled flaming from the coals.

There was little talk. For the moment it seemed right to sit back and soak in the silence. Pierre watched the fire fall to embers as the full dark came on. The night air was heavy with the scents of wild berry blossoms and birch catkins. The far-off music of the rapids drifting down over the camp made it easy for Pierre to forget his blisters.

It was La Londe who broke the spell. "Captain," he said across the fire to McKay, "it's amazing what a powerful thirst a day's paddling can bring."

"Would you like to borrow my cup then," McKay said, "to fetch a good draft from the river?"

"To tell the truth, I was thinking of something a bit more lively."

"More lively than the Ottawa?" McKay shrugged his shoulders.

La Londe was quiet until Bellegarde and Michel Larocque, the wiry little middleman who helped the bowman lead his songs, appeared a minute later. Each man had a keg of brandy under his arm, and Bellegarde proudly announced, "Mr. McKay has ordered the liquor ration for the trip issued."

The crew cheered, and La Londe said, "We drink to Commander McKay." Pierre was amazed at how quickly the men crowded around Bellegarde, with their cups already in hand. The day he'd worked in the storehouse with La Petite, the big man explained that a few ounces of liquor were allotted to each man in the brigade. It was just enough for some small celebrating, but no *voyageur* would ever head north without his ration of brandy.

McKay nodded politely to the men and then retired to his tent. As he walked past Pierre, the commander noticed the boy's frown. "I'm not being unsociable, lad, I'm just not a drinking man. The company says to issue liquor, so I give them their dram of poison early in the trip, and then I'm done with it."

Pierre and Charbonneau were the only others to abstain. Charbonneau said he'd sworn off spirits several summers past, and everyone assumed Grandpa was too young. As Pierre took a seat on an aspen log, Beloît teased him. "Is our little lady friend afraid to taste something stronger than mother's milk?"

Charbonneau reached out a hand to hold Pierre back, but it was too late. He was up and digging in his pack for a cup. The first sip of brandy nearly gagged him. It burned his throat and nose and made his eyes water, but he choked down a few more swigs. If he couldn't paddle like a *voyageur,* at least he could drink like one.

The men celebrated at the same frantic pace as they paddled and ate. Clustering around the fire, they sang bawdy songs and took turns telling stories. A short while later Larocque stepped forward and announced, "It is time for the test."

Several men stood to take on his challenge. To Pierre's surprise, the test was jumping over the campfire. The men leaped over the fire the short way and then the long. Others joined in, laughing and clapping their friends on the back as they braved the flames.

But after the fourth round of drinks, Larocque decided to make his "course," as he called it, more challenging. He piled fresh wood on the roaring fire and waited until the flames were crackling high. Then he leaped. He singed his leggings a bit, but others were quick to accept the new challenge.

When La Londe took his turn, Pierre asked Charbonneau, "Why does La Londe have such white hair? He doesn't look that old."

"He isn't. All I can say for sure," Charbonneau said, "is that it happened one summer about ten years back. He left for the English River with hair the same sort of blond as yours, and when he came back, his head was pure white."

"He wouldn't say what happened?"

"It wasn't my place to ask. But I met a fellow once who was up on the English that summer. There was an accident. He claimed a north canoe capsized in a rapids just after the ice melted. Seven men drowned. La Londe was the only one to survive. But there's no telling for sure."

Just then there was a shout. Pierre turned to see Jean Beloît trip La Londe as he leaped out over the fire. His body twisted sideways, and he landed on his shoulder in the coals. A roll set him clear. His leather shirt saved his back, and Emile and Bellegarde saved his hair by throwing a blanket over his head while he lay, half stunned, in the sand.

Bellegarde brushed La Londe off and helped him to his feet. Then, before anyone could blink, La Londe yelled, "You dog," and leaped for Beloît's throat. La Londe's hair was still smoking as the two men went down. They grappled and punched with a fury that looked certain to end in death.

A circle formed, and everyone cheered his favorite. "Beloît will kill him," Emile said. By his tone Pierre could tell he was disappointed that the reverse wasn't true.

"Come on La Londe, get him," Pierre yelled, fearing this good-humored fellow would get hurt. Pierre clenched his fist and swung at the air. He wished he could pummel the evil Beloît himself.

The crewmen alternately cheered and sipped their brandy. A man offered to fill Pierre's cup, but he shook his head. Pierre already felt dizzy from the strong drink, and when he tried to focus on the grappling fighters, their faces blurred together. Twice La Londe and Beloît rolled dangerously close to the fire, but Bellegarde rolled them away. When it was clear neither man could gain an advantage, Charbonneau said, "Let's give Beloît a dram of his own poison."

"A little singe will do him good," Bellegarde agreed. The next time Beloît rolled toward the fire, everyone stepped aside. It took Beloît a while to realize his moccasin was on fire. When the pain finally hit him, he let out a shout and rolled his opponent into the brush.

Bellowing like a wounded bull, he kicked off his smoking moccasin and leaped feetfirst into the shallows.

Pierre expected Beloît to return with a knife, but the man was grinning when he came back from the river. He walked up to La Londe and shook his hand. "Well fought, *hivernant,*" he said.

La Londe returned the compliment. "You gave me more than I wanted, Jean."

They embraced, and while Beloît sat down in the sand and wrapped his burned foot in his red cap, La Londe poured his opponent a drink.

"Is it like this all the time?" Pierre asked Charbonneau.

"Sometimes"—he smiled—"but it's the first few nights mainly that get so wild. When the tension of waiting all winter to get back at their paddles mixes with the brandy"—he waved toward La Londe and Beloît sitting side by side—"there you have it."

A few men had already crawled under the nearest canoe and retired for the night, so Charbonneau and Pierre decided to do the same. "It's best we take a good place," the veteran advised. "The air gets chilly in the open this time of the year."

They found a Montréal a few paces from the campfire and laid their blankets under the hull. Pierre was exhausted, but sleep did not come easily. The ground was lumpy, and every turn forced his hip or elbow against a rock. Even worse, Charbonneau was already snoring on one side, while Beloît and La Londe kept chatting just up the bank. Pierre suddenly had a terrible headache, too.

"You know that island," Beloît said, "the one just this side of the rapids?"

"What about it?"

"When I was down there on the bank, staring out into the moonlight, I swore I was looking on Massacre Island—the one up on Rainy River where the priest and eighteen of La Vérendrye's men were murdered. My old partner Joseph Le Clair was in the party that found 'em. It was plenty ugly. He said the bodies were spread out on buffalo robes in a circle with their heads—most of 'em scalped—piled up in the middle. Some had knife cuts in patterns all over their backs. Others had porcupine quills stuck in their legs. They left the priest in the center with his right hand stuck straight up in the air and an arrow in his side. His head was split clear open."

La Londe whistled softly, and then it was quiet.

A short while later La Londe crawled under the far

end of the canoe, and Beloît lay right down on the open ground. They both began snoring immediately.

Pierre turned over again and again, but sleep wouldn't come.

When he finally drifted off, he dreamed that his father and mother and his sisters were lying in a circle on a huge buffalo robe with their arms over their heads. Their faces were smiling as bravely as they had this morning when they said goodbye. But next to a silver hatchet in the center of the circle lay Beloît's cap, heaped to the top with severed thumbs.

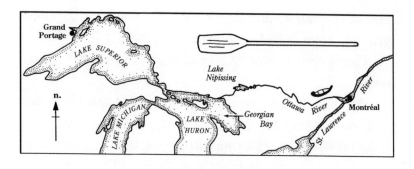

CHAPTER 6

$\blacksquare\diamond\blacksquare$

First Light

IN THE BACK of his mind Pierre heard a low growling, then the sound of claws digging into tree bark. I must be dreaming, he thought, pulling his blanket tighter around his shoulders. His head ached even worse than it had the night before. He was just drifting back to sleep when a second growl came.

A bear.

Pierre's eyes flashed opened. Crouched at the base of a pine was André Bellegarde, scratching the bark with his bear claw necklace.

"Ha, Ha," Beloît cackled from behind. He trotted to Pierre's side and leaned directly over his face. "Portage time," he croaked, his black eyes glittering. "Say goodbye to your pretty dreams."

Beloît's breath smelled of stale liquor, and his mutilated nose was even uglier than Pierre remembered it.

"Go away," Pierre said, but Beloît and Bellegarde picked up the canoe that had been Pierre's shelter for the night. Pierre blinked as bits of leaves and sand fell onto his face.

While the men carried the canoe away, Pierre focused his sleep-swollen eyes. It was still dark, but the canoes were all gone. The few men who remained in camp were picking up parcels from the pile at the end of the beach and starting up the trail.

Pierre scrambled to his feet. He stuffed his blanket into his pack and hurried over to help with the work. His muscles were sore, and his right hand was raw and aching.

"It's time to work, Graybeard," Beloît greeted him when he got to the pile of parcels. "We were ready to leave you for bear bait."

Mr. McKay said, "Good afternoon, lad. I hope you weren't waiting for us to bring you breakfast in bed." Pierre's cheeks were hot. His head pounded. His lips felt dry and cracked, and his mouth tasted as if it were filled with sawdust.

Beloît helped La Londe hoist his double packs in place. La Londe paused a moment to adjust his tumpline and wink at Pierre. He patted the boy on the shoulder and grinned. "It's an easy carry, son," he said, trotting off with his usual springy stride.

"I think we start you with one pack today." Beloît reached for a parcel. His hair was still plastered with bits of sand and leaves from sleeping on the ground. Pierre tried not to look at his face.

"No, give me the same as everyone," Pierre insisted, anxious to get away from Beloît as fast as he could.

"Whatever you say." Beloît heaved the first pack onto his back.

The straps cut into Pierre's shoulders and jerked him backward. He wheeled his arms to keep from falling.

Beloît grinned. "Ready for another?"

Pierre gasped as he tottered to maintain his balance, "I'll come back for the other one."

"As you wish," Beloît snickered, taking two packs for himself as Pierre started up the path.

The trail was rugged. As Pierre stepped from one rock to the next, he tried not to imagine how embarrassing it would be to trip while carrying only a single pack.

Before he was halfway up the ridge, La Petite passed him, stepping out into the bushes and back onto the trail without breaking stride. Three bundles were stacked on his back. Pierre multiplied three times ninety in his mind, and couldn't believe La Petite carried that much weight without even slowing down. Beloît and another man, both portaging double packs, passed Pierre before he reached the crown of the spruce-covered hill.

The straps cut into his shirt as if they were sharp metal bands, and there was no way to relieve the pain. If he leaned into the tumpline to take the weight off his back, his neck muscles burned and his body pitched forward. If he hooked his thumbs under the straps to relieve the weight, his blisters grated against the canvas.

Thankful for his strong legs, Pierre barely felt the load on his lower body until he was well over the rise. But as he worked his way down the backside of the ridge, he suddenly wondered if he would make it. The muscles in his legs popped out with each step, and his calves burned.

Knowing he was the last one on the trail, he thought for moment about tossing his pack into the brush. He could hike home in a day and be done with the pain for good.

When Pierre noticed a mossy patch of ground ahead, he decided to rest a minute. But just then he saw a bright patch of blue through the underbrush. Water. He held his pace, knowing that if the path turned rough again he would never make it.

The trail took a sharp turn to the left and suddenly got steeper. Pierre groaned. But there was no stopping now.

Partway down the hill he looked up. The entire crew stood at attention below, facing him. Pierre heard taunts and jeers inside his head, yet the men just stared, strangely silent. As Pierre leaned into the tumpline, he saw La Petite whisper something to La Londe. Both men grinned.

I'll show them, he silently vowed. Throwing caution aside, he doubled his pace, risking a headlong tumble.

His legs gave out as he reached the shore. La Petite caught him under the arms as the weight of Pierre's pack twisted his body around and jerked him backward. His feet flew up, and he nearly rolled into the river.

Suddenly the men cheered. La Petite helped Pierre out of his pack straps and onto his feet. Several men stepped forward and clapped him on the back. He was confused even more when Charbonneau stepped forward and shook his hand saying, "Fine carry, son."

"Good job, lad." McKay tipped his hat.

"You showed 'em," La Londe said, and Emile, who had thrown his cap in the air, patted Pierre on the shoulder. Pierre's head throbbed, and he was confused by all the attention.

It wasn't until Pierre saw Beloît toss a coin to La Petite that he finally figured things out. Pierre knelt to examine his pack. He lifted the flap, and a handful of musket balls rolled out.

Someone had stuffed his pack with bags of lead shot. He wondered how many had bet against his making it. Pierre took one of the heavy balls in his hand and stood up. His knuckles went white as he squeezed the bullet in his palm. How stupid could he be?

"A lucky carry," Beloît said, spitting into the rocks at Pierre's feet as he stepped toward the waiting canoes. "A man-sized portage would've flattened him."

"I told them you'd make it," La Petite said, "but they refused to believe. Their doubt has cost them dearly." He paused and rattled the newly won coins in his palm. "If that pack weighed an ounce, it weighed two hundred pounds."

The musket ball dropped from Pierre's hand onto the black rocks. "You mean it weighs as much as a double pack?"

"Without a doubt, my young *voyageur.*"

"Young, I'll believe," Beloît snarled as he turned to climb in his canoe. "As for *voyageur?* We shall see." But Pierre was looking at his pack, amazed at what he'd done.

La Petite gave Pierre one more clap on the back and waded out to his canoe. The big man collected on a few more wagers after he had taken his place in the stern. He turned toward Pierre one last time, raising his leather coin pouch high and jingling it by its drawstrings. "See me at the next portage, Pierre," he called. "I give you a share of the winnings."

"I've got a little something for you, too," La Londe said, waving his paddle at Pierre. "We pick our ponies pretty well, eh, partner?" he bragged to the men in the other canoes. "If we get much luckier we'll have to give up our voyaging and open a bank."

Despite the chorus of boos from middlemen who'd lost money in the betting, Charbonneau's canoe was under way a moment later. As they started upriver, La Londe took up an old French folksong:

Behold the fair Françoise,
Behold the fair Françoise,
She would wed if she may, maluron, lurette,
She would wed if she may, maluron, lurette,

Her love comes late a-calling,
Her love comes . . .

At the chorus Pierre joined in, pulling as hard on his paddle as his blisters would allow. He was glad to have his first portage behind him, but he was uneasy about the carries that lay ahead.

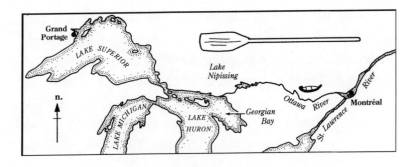

CHAPTER 7

The Long Sault

AN HOUR LATER the brigade reached a second rapids. They
"tracked" this stretch of water, pulling each craft up the
rapids with a sixty-yard line. One man stood in the bow
and two in the stern, using setting poles to steady the
canoe in the swift current. The rest of the crew danced
from one slippery rock to the next, as they hauled their
five-thousand-pound load upstream.

Fed by ice fields in the north, the Ottawa ran deep and
cold. Since Pierre was hot and sweaty from paddling, the
chilly water felt good at first, but after only a few steps he
lost the feeling in his feet, and the wet tracking rope cut
into his right hand.

Near the head of the rapids, just as La Londe and Charbonneau were poling hard to swing the long birch bark hull clear of a menacing boulder, Pierre slipped and wet himself to the waist. His high-pitched squeal gave the crew good reason to chuckle. As Pierre scrambled back to shore, Charbonneau called out in mock anger, "No swimming on company time, La Page. There's work to be done."

"Be careful, Tadpole." Bellegarde chortled from the bank. "There's some hungry turtles in this stream." The crew roared.

Pierre scowled. He was freezing cold and feeling sorry for himself. He could easily have been swept downstream and drowned, yet they were laughing as if he were a circus clown. But when he saw La Londe grinning at him, Pierre looked down at his soaked pants and his skinny blue ankles. Realizing how silly he must look, he couldn't help chuckling along.

As they pushed out into a broad pool at the head of the rapids, Pierre studied the river bottom. White sand and bright, quartz-flecked pebbles glowed in the shallows; just where the bottom fell off into sudden blackness, he saw the speckled tail of a huge brook trout.

As soon as they hit the open river, the paddlers fell into a stroke-a-second pace. Pierre's sore hand began to ache. He tried hard to keep up, hearing his father's words: "You'll find no better friends than your canoe mates if you do your part."

* * *

The day grew hot. Pierre's skin itched as his pants dried in the sun. Blue flies, excited by the blood smell from Pierre's hand, buzzed over the canoe.

The heat made Pierre dizzy. He felt almost as sick as he had two winters ago, when an earache came on so suddenly that he cried. He was fine one minute. Then his head began to pound, and he felt as if someone was shoving a hot pin into his ear. He got so feverish that his eyes wouldn't focus, and according to his mother, he started to say silly things, rambling on about his aunt Millie and a pig and a silver snuffbox. Though Mother and Camille bathed his forehead with cool rags all night, the pain didn't go away until the middle of the next morning, when his eardrum burst. Though Mother was afraid he'd be deaf in that ear, his hearing gradually came back.

Just then a deerfly bit Pierre between the fingers of his right hand, and he dropped his paddle to dig at the throbbing bite. "What's the matter?" Beloît teased. "Does our puppy have fleas?"

Pierre flushed, but he made no comment, as the crewmen on all sides had another laugh. Just once he wished he could dunk Beloît's ugly face in the river. He tried not to scratch, but that made the itching more maddening. Pierre envied the older men their long hair, which kept the flies off their necks and shoulders.

Luckily, there was more bull work this morning than

paddling. If he was careful with the tracking lines, his cuts might start to heal.

Just after they'd tracked their canoe up a tight chute bordered by lichen-covered rock ledges, Charbonneau gave Pierre advice that didn't seem to make sense. "If the paddling seems hard, Pierre," he said, "it is only because you make it so. To paddle properly you must forget you are paddling."

Pierre frowned as the steersman continued. "It may sound crazy, but it works."

"Tell these blisters they don't hurt," Pierre said. Charbonneau's tone angered him. The man seemed to think that all it took was an order to make a thing happen.

"The pain will pass!" Charbonneau snapped impatiently. "I must warn you. We hit the big water soon. To paddle fifteen hours a day, the head and the heart must be strong."

When they stopped to recoil their lines a little later, La Londe took Pierre aside. "Listen to your steersman," he gently urged. "The truth is a strange dog sometimes, but work is only as hard as we make it. Focus on a special place—a Christmas long ago, the bonnet of a pretty girl— and your paddle becomes a small thing."

He admired La Londe's calm. Pierre could tell the bowman encouraged him to try it for his own good, where Charbonneau only worried about how many miles the brigade could make. When they took up their paddles again, Pierre tried to follow his advice. He studied the pines along the riverbank, but his hands still hurt. He recalled his last time with Celeste, but even as he imagined her bright blue eyes, his ears burned at the memory of his awkwardness.

The more he thought about the advice, the more foolish it sounded. He'd never made a job easy by forgetting. Forgetting made his mother angry. How many times had he been sent out after supper to finish a chore he'd forgotten? "It isn't fair for the chickens to go hungry because you're lazy," she'd say.

The brigade finally stopped for breakfast at the base of a rapids. There was a short but steep portage. As the canoes coasted up to the landing, Pierre noticed that each man briefly doffed his cap. He looked up and saw a series of faded red crosses standing on top of the hill. He'd heard about these crosses left in memory of *voyageurs* who'd drowned, but he'd never seen one.

After the men unloaded, Pierre studied the white trough that roared down the boulder-strewn channel. He was awed that anyone would ever attempt such a run.

He looked back up the hill and asked La Londe, "How many crosses are there?"

"Nineteen as of last fall."

"That many died right here?"

La Londe nodded. In the pool below the rapids, Pierre watched a beaver-gnawed stick bobbing in the foam. It was easy to imagine a dead man, facedown in the flotsam, spinning in a slow circle.

"Why would anyone ever want to try those rapids?"

"It's a tough carry," was all La Londe said.

"*Voyageurs* don't try it anymore, do they?"

"It is forbidden by the company." The flat tone of La Londe's voice hinted that this was a policy not always obeyed.

Pierre pictured himself alone in a canoe hurtling down the white channel, flailing with his paddle. "You've never run it, have you?"

There was a long pause. When La Londe finally spoke, his eyes were fixed on the red crosses. "It's a tough carry," he repeated.

Breakfast was the same as dinner and the same as every meal would be for the next six weeks—boiled corn and salt pork. Pierre nibbled at the first bite and only then realized his hunger. He devoured his heaping plateful, not caring whether it was corn or oats or hay. Food helped drive the paddles, and he needed strength.

When it was time to portage, Pierre carefully inspected both his parcels. Catching him with his hand beneath the pack flaps, La Petite teased, "What you fishing for, Pierre? I think you have better luck if you try the river."

"You know what I'm looking for, La Petite," Pierre said. "No one's tricking me again with an overloaded pack."

"So, I will have to find another pony to place my wagers on?"

"That's right."

"Well, here's your slice of the pie." With a big laugh that echoed up the rocky channel, he tossed Pierre a coin purse.

Then, as Pierre was getting ready to hoist up his pack, La Londe took him by the arm. "And here's a little present from me."

La Londe, his blue eyes lit with excitement, handed Pierre a sheath knife. The handle was carved caribou horn, and it had a moosehide sheath decorated with colored beading.

"I couldn't take such a fine—"

"You deserve it. You won that wager for us."

"But this is too much," Pierre protested.

"I promised you a share. Besides, I made it myself. It's a winter hobby of mine. A knife means more to a boy than a sack of coins, right?"

Pierre nodded, awed by the gleam of the honed edge.

"Besides, we white-hairs got to stick together," La Londe grinned, ruffling Pierre's hair. "Just don't cut your hand off. Your mother would skin my hide."

When Pierre had both ninety-pound parcels in place, he was amazed at how light they felt. The balance was so much better than the pack they'd tricked him with. That one rode low on his hips and put a strain on his back and neck. These sat high and let him carry the weight with his legs.

The rest of the day passed quietly in a mix of brief

paddling stints and work with the tracking lines. Most of the men were suffering from the previous night's celebration, and they looked peaked. Beloît, complaining so loudly that the whole brigade could hear, claimed his mouth tasted "like the inside of a British boot."

The only excitement occurred late in the day, when La Petite's bowman suddenly drew out his North West gun and fired toward the near shore. There was a furious flapping of wings, and after the smoke from the musket charge drifted downriver, Pierre saw a duck floating on the water. The canoemen cheered when the man tossed his kill to the cook, André Bellegarde.

"Meat for the cooking pot," La Londe called out.

Emile, grinning hungrily, yelled, "Duck soup!"

Bellegarde stood up in his canoe, limp carcass in hand, and bowed dramatically to his benefactor. "Fine shooting, *monsieur*," he said.

CHAPTER 8

Night of the Kettle Dance

THAT NIGHT THE brigade camped at the head of the Long Sault. Though Pierre was glad to have those tough portages behind him, he was nervous when Charbonneau bragged about how far they would paddle the next day: "Tomorrow we hit a sweet stretch of river—not a single shoal or rapids to slow us down. We cover forty miles easy."

That meant steady paddling with his blistered hands. As they carried the packs up to the campsite, Pierre asked Emile, "Can we really paddle that far in one day?"

"Charbonneau starts fast," Emile said with a smile, tugging at his curly sideburns, "and once we hit the big water, he'll go even faster." He looked at Pierre's hands. "How they holding up?"

Pierre shrugged. He didn't want to admit that his fingers were too sore to straighten.

While the light was still strong, Pierre helped Emile gum the canoe and fix the wattape, the cedar root lacing on the canoe seams that had frayed during their upstream drags. Every canoe carried spare wattape and pine gum, as well as a rolled sheet of birch bark for repairing leaks and tears.

Later Pierre wandered down to the shore and looked north. Above the horizon rose the forbidding, glacier-scoured hills of the Canadian Shield. "So what do you think of her?" La Londe asked. He relaxed on a nearby log.

"It looks like tough country."

"Tough and wild," La Londe agreed. "That ridge will lie to the north for our whole trip to Grand Portage."

Pierre nodded. His father had told him of the famous outcroppings known as the Laurentian Hills. They marked the point where the rivers started flowing north to Hudson Bay.

"When the first explorers came searching for a trade route to China, that highland crushed their hopes, but to us it's home."

"Home?" Pierre questioned, staring at the cold hills.

La Londe laughed at Pierre's frown. "I remember the first night I camped here. I was scared stiff. A fourteen-year-old short-hair away from home for the very first time, I sat down on that ledge right over there and bawled my eyes out."

Pierre frowned. He wondered if La Londe was making up a story to make him feel good.

"It's true," La Londe insisted, seeing the doubt in Pierre's eyes. "That spring my old man booted me out of the house. One day he said, 'Time you got out and made something of yourself.' Next thing you know, my papers were signed, and I was paddling north."

"Your father never asked if you wanted to sign on?"

"No." La Londe laughed at Pierre's astonishment. "He was a storekeeper, and nine kids were too many to feed. So out I went."

"Just like that?"

"There's no need to feel sorry for me," he said, patting Pierre gently on the shoulder. "I headed north that year, and I never did go back. In a season I fell in love with this life. Wouldn't trade it for anything now. Besides"—La Londe smiled as he stood and waved a hand in the direction of the men who were clustered around the campfire—"who could ever ask for a nicer family than those fellows?"

Alone, Pierre watched the sun disappear in pink and purple trails. Cold crept down from the darkening hills, and steam rose off the water. A blackbird called upriver.

Pierre thought of his mother back home in Lachine. She would be warming a pot of tea on the woodstove about now. From the time he was a little boy he'd taken a cup of tea with his parents before he went to bed. When he was small the tea was mostly milk, but it made him feel like a grown-up. Later there was a book or a story before they tucked him in for the night.

When Pierre walked back to camp, he found Belle-garde at the fire, preparing the evening's "feast." The big cooking pot, filled with water, pork fat, and corn, was propped between two flat rocks and just beginning to steam. The air was heavy with smoke. Bellegarde knelt, whistling, making quick work of the duck. He tossed feathers in all directions. Pierre smiled when he imagined what his mother would think of the cook's crude technique.

It was hard for Pierre not to stare at the cook's scarred face. Bellegarde was a thin man with greasy hair and small, close-set eyes. He was the oldest man in the brigade and, according to La Petite, the most experienced, having traveled down the Fraser River to Canada's western coast. His work as a cook was "a step toward retirement."

"Is it true," Pierre asked, "that you've canoed to Athabasca?"

"It is," Bellegarde replied, never taking his eyes off the duck. "And true that I've paddled all the way to the Pacific. And true that I've spent many a winter with nothing but a trading gun to bring down my supper."

"You wintered that far west?"

"I've traveled twice to New Caledonia, and I've married eight good wives, too. I surely haven't wasted my whole life with pork-eaters such as these," he said, jerking his head and spitting into the fire. Men who went no farther north than Grand Portage were sometimes called pork-eaters, out of scorn.

"I've seen sights that'd turn your blood cold," he stated, as he laid the duck across a log and sawed off its head and feet with his hunting knife.

Next Bellegarde crouched before the fire and passed the bird back and forth through the flames a few times to singe off the pinfeathers. Then, in a voice loud enough for half the camp to hear, he announced, "Now to flavor our soup."

To Pierre's horror, Bellegarde tossed the blackened carcass, entrails and all, into the cooking pot. Pierre coughed, and the cook turned with a grin. "What's this, young man? Is my butchering not fancy enough for you?"

"So, Bellegarde," Charbonneau interrupted from the far side of the fire, "which one of your wives taught you such a recipe for duck? I bet she was old and blind."

A chorus of laughs rose around the fire.

"She was lots prettier than you fellows," Bellegarde scoffed, "and she could see plenty good."

Pierre stared at Bellegarde, wondering what else he planned to throw into his kettle. Jean Beloît, who was sitting on a flat rock, teased Pierre. "You never want to waste the guts, boy. That's the tastiest part."

Beloît saw Pierre grimace, so he pushed it one step further. "Just ask the Sioux. Those fellows love the innards. After a buffalo kill they'll fight for the first bite of raw liver. Same with the intestines. I've seen braves chew their way through a gut pile like kids at a taffy pull."

Wide-eyed, he raked his hands through an imaginary mound of entrails. "There's hundreds of feet," he continued, "and it stretches so far that a man can start at either end and . . ."

When Pierre jumped up, Beloît feigned surprise. "What's wrong?"

As Pierre knelt behind a big balsam tree and emptied his stomach, he could hear Beloît bragging, "I think something make little Grandpa sick."

Pierre hated that stupid cackling voice. He heard La Londe stick up for him. "What'd you do to the poor boy, let him look at you? That'd make anybody sick."

Pierre felt ashamed. As bad as the nickname "Grandpa" was, "poor boy" was even worse.

Later, when the men gathered around the kettle to fill their plates, Pierre walked back toward the fire. McKay took his place at the head of the line, and the other crewmen fell in behind him. Though Pierre didn't feel like eating, he knew he could never endure forty miles of upstream paddling tomorrow without food. It was a mystery to him how these men could work so hard, living on only two meals and pipe smoke.

He took a place near the end of the line, trying to draw as little attention to himself as possible. When his turn finally came, Bellegarde ladled a big pile of soupy corn onto his plate.

Just when it looked as if Pierre would be left to eat in peace, Beloît crowed, "I see why they call this one Grandpa. He wiser than his years. How many young fellows be smart enough to know the best comes last? It's a clever fellow who waits until the pot is almost empty and the duck parts are settled to the bottom."

Pierre just smiled and set down his food without looking at it. "Here," he said to Bellegarde, "let me help. It's not fair that the cook always has to eat last."

Astonished by such unexpected consideration, Bellegarde accepted Pierre's offer. As Pierre loaded up Bellegarde's plate, the proud cook turned toward the fire, declaring to anyone who would listen, "Finally we have a man among us who knows how to treat André."

Pierre served the rest of the men. When it was Beloît's turn, he pointed to the boy's ladle. "Look," he said, "our little lady friend has found a tool he can handle." Pierre's ears burned, but he said nothing.

Beloît laughed his way to a seat on a rock next to La Londe and began eating. Pierre watched Beloît as he served the last men. It took him longer to eat than the others, because he talked the whole time. Bits of food fell into his lap or got caught in his beard, but he didn't care.

Just when Pierre was convinced that Beloît would never finish his meal, the man took a big scoop from his borrowed plate, saying, "This is what I call corn soup. It tastes like poetry, it does."

"Look who's talking," Charbonneau said. "You wouldn't know a poem from a pack sack."

Beloît shoveled the heaping spoonful in and bit down hard. But suddenly he was spitting the food onto the ground. "Achh," he growled, hacking and spitting a second time.

"What's the matter?" La Londe asked. "Can't you stomach that elegant meat?" The rest of the crew turned to see what had caused the commotion.

Beloît searched the ground frantically. A moment later he paused and slowly held up the bright orange foot of a duck.

"Who's had his hands in the cooking pot?"

Several men grinned, but no one said anything. "I'll have his ears, I will," Beloît said. As he spoke, he fingered the hilt of the knife that hung at his waist.

Pierre could no longer contain himself and burst into a peal of laughter. Beloît rubbed his eyes and squinted. "You?"

The whole company joined in Pierre's laughter. La Londe, his white hair shaking, clapped Beloît on the shoulder, saying, "That's one on you, *hivernant*."

Beloît glared across the fire, still touching the bone

handle of his knife. Pierre imagined what his ears would look like floating in the cooking pot.

"What's the matter, Jean?" Charbonneau called. "I've heard the Sioux regard duck's feet as a rare delicacy."

That was enough to bring a half smile to Beloît's face. As he grinned, he tossed the webbed foot toward Pierre, saying, "You such a good cook's helper, I share it with you."

"Thank you, sir," Pierre said in mock politeness as the foot rolled to the edge of the fire, "but I've had my fill."

When Beloît laughed again, Pierre knew he was safe, but his heart was racing as if he'd run a long way. What would he have done if the evil man had unsheathed his knife?

He finally sat down to eat. The corn and duck and salt pork were delicious, sweetened by his revenge.

Pierre was ready for bed. He needed rest if he wanted to survive the next day's paddling with his aching arms and blistered hands. But just as Pierre was reaching for his blanket, La Petite shouted, "It's time for the kettle dance," and there was a great commotion throughout the camp.

Without another word, kegs were opened and two sacks were placed beside the fire. La Petite, as a senior member of the brigade, stood on one sack, while Emile Duval stood on the other. Each held a kettle under his arm.

Pierre watched as Emile, dressed in deerskin leggings, a long shirt, a sash, and a feathered cap, began prancing in a half circle and singing:

We leave, good hearts, our loves behind,
For a parting to span three seasons.
But voyageurs born, we journey to live,
And spit in the face of danger.

Duval paused then, and the rest of the crew took up the rousing chorus:

We start the bold traverse today,
Away, brave friends, away.
For the safety of our company pray.
Away, brave friends, away.

La Petite stepped forward, dressed in a blue cloak and red sash. Carrying a beaded bag, he moved about slowly and sang in a big, sweet voice:

Dark will our nights be and cold our couches.
The devil, by day, will seize our blades.
Over portages long, and saults and streams,
With death-stalked hearts we sing.

The crew joined in as before, and the singers went on, taking turns for the next seven verses. The men laughed and clapped, and at the end of each verse, at least one man shrieked.

Pierre, trying to shake the sleep from his eyes, studied the cavorting men and thought back over the hard upstream haul they'd made that day. Where does all their energy come from? he wondered, admiring La Londe's high-kicking style.

When Pierre was too tired to watch any longer, he rolled out his blanket under a canoe. The voices soon faded as he fell into a deep, dreamless sleep.

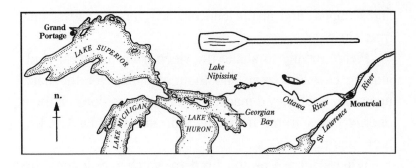

CHAPTER 9

◆

A Long Day's Paddle

THE BRIGADE WAS up again at four A.M., and with the Long Sault behind them, the *voyageurs* were in great spirits. While Mr. McKay was still in his tent getting dressed, La Londe grinned and said, "Watch this." Pierre's eyes widened as La Londe sneaked behind McKay's tent and released the support poles. To everyone's delight, the tent collapsed. Unbothered, McKay crawled out the door opening and stood with his pants at half-mast.

Pulling his suspenders up, he eyed the likely culprit. "Top of the morning to you, gentlemen," the big Scotsman said, making no effort to hide his grin. "It cheers my heart to see ye all so anxious to get under way."

"That we are, sir," La Londe replied, "and awaiting your good guidance." With that they all had a good laugh. Pierre chuckled until his belly felt warm.

The prospect of a daylong paddle was frightening, but the good humor of the morning relaxed him. And as they started upriver, La Petite and La Londe led the men in song. Old French sea chants, folksongs, and silly rhymes echoed up and down the river as Pierre dug in with his paddle.

The sun warmed Pierre's shoulders as it rose, illuminating the left-hand shore and finally the river. Thin trails of mist lifted off the water. Birds rustled through the dry leaves on the near bank. A stilt-legged heron stalked his breakfast in a reed bed.

Pierre tried to follow his bowman's advice. He sang along with the men. He studied the stately pines and the distant ridges. He imagined where the blue Ottawa would eventually lead them, but his hands still throbbed. Forgetting the effort of paddling by losing himself to other thoughts sounded simple, but his hands were so puffed and swollen that he felt as if chunks of skin were pulling loose from them.

He thought about school, imagining Celeste in her seat by the window. He saw the morning sun shining on her silky black hair and her blue dress, patterned with tiny white flowers. About now Sister Marguérite was standing before the class, saying, "Take your places now, children."

Closing his eyes for an instant, Pierre could smell the chalk dust and the freshly oiled maple floor and the damp winter clothing drying on a line behind the stove. He could hear Sister reading her favorite Bible verse: "Lay not up for yourselves treasures upon earth, where moth and rust doth corrupt, and where thieves . . ."

When the brigade stopped for breakfast, La Londe checked on Pierre's hands. "So how's the paws holding up today?" he asked, reaching out to inspect a hand.

"Whew," he whistled, studying the oozing blisters. "Looks like you been leaning on a hot griddle. These are almost as bad as mine were on my first trip out. My hands blistered up and bled so bad that I whined constantly. The fellows threatened to throw me in for fish bait." La Londe laughed. "Let me show you a little trick."

While breakfast was cooking, the bowman took some deerhide strips out of his pack. "It's doeskin—the softest stuff you could ever find," he said. Then he took Pierre's paddle and wrapped the handle with several turns. "There, that should help—"

"What's this?" Beloît interrupted. "Does our puppy need padding for his little hands?"

Pierre looked away, but the ugly man stepped closer and examined the newly wrapped paddle. "If I'd only known," he continued in mock concern, "my mother has some pretty silk gloves she could have loaned—"

La Londe cut him off, saying, "Stick your ugly puss in somebody else's business."

As Beloît walked off cackling, La Londe said, "Consider the source. Don't let him get to you." But Pierre hated Jean Beloît more and more every day. He stared after him. If only he could crack the crude fellow over the head with his paddle. One hard swing was all he wanted. Pierre smiled to himself as he imagined the cedar blade splintering over the brute's head. He was sure the other crewmen would cheer, and even if Beloît stabbed him in the heart, Pierre would die content.

The padded handle helped, but the pain was still severe. Shortly after breakfast, it began to rain. Pierre pulled his cap over his ears and hunched down, but the other men all pulled their shirts off and stuffed them under the oilcloth tarp that protected the freight.

Steam rose off the naked shoulders of the crew. Pierre watched the rain bead up on dark-skinned Emile, who was sitting directly in front of him. As the rain increased, water coursed down his back. Charbonneau leaned toward Pierre, saying, "If it wasn't too late I'd tell you to shed your clothing."

"What good would that do?" Pierre asked.

"You'll see shortly," Emile said, turning. His expression made Pierre nervous, for though Emile had only been in the brigades for two years, he knew a lot about the *voyageur* life.

A short while later Pierre understood Emile's grin. Though the other men paddled freely, his soaked shirt made it hard for him to lift his arms. The heavy fabric clung to his shoulders, and his collar channeled a river down his back and into his pants.

Soon he began to itch. He twisted on his seat between paddle strokes, and Charbonneau chuckled. "What is the trouble, *monsieur?*" he asked. "Have you wet your britches, perhaps?"

When the sun came out, the other men put their shirts back on, but Pierre took his off and draped it over the gunwale to dry. The flies swarmed over him. One bit him on the shoulder and two more left big welts in the middle of his back.

"You must have sweet blood," Charbonneau remarked. "The flies sing like they've found a honey pot."

Though it didn't make sense, the pain of his bites made him forget the pain of his paddling. He didn't even know what had happened until their next rest stop. Pierre put his hand on the gunwale and got a jolt of pain. The blisters were raw, but he couldn't remember when he'd last felt them.

Could those old-timers be right after all? Pierre wondered as he stepped onto the beach.

While the crewmen lit their pipes and rested, Pierre stretched his legs and studied his swollen hands.

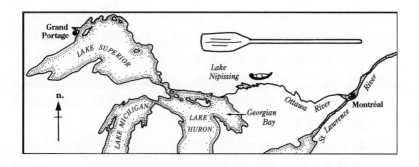

CHAPTER 10

The Confluence of the Mattawa

THE DAYS ON the Ottawa River passed in a rushing blur. Life for Pierre was reduced to water and sky and the churning paddles of the bright-prowed canoes.

"It will get easier before you know it, Pierre," La Londe insisted more times than the boy could count. But for Pierre the days got longer and harder. A cold front moved in, and each morning there was a heavy coating of frost on the canoes and a rim of ice at the river's edge. The *voyageurs* woke up cursing the cold as they brushed ice crystals from their mustaches.

The bright chill reminded Pierre of a Christmas when Father took him and Camille on a sleigh ride. Father hitched their plow horse to an old wooden sledge, and as they started up a spruce-lined trail, Camille and Pierre cheered. On the way home they sang loud carols and giggled when Father drove so fast that the snow stung their cheeks and Camille's hair blew straight back and tickled Pierre's nose.

La Londe reminded Pierre of the joy his father had shown that Christmas long ago. Every day was a holiday to La Londe. No matter how much the rest of the crew complained, he stayed cheerful. "There's no finer weather than this," he preached to Pierre. "No bugs. No rain. Bright mornings made for hard paddling."

Just when Pierre was convinced he would see no relief from the cold, the weather suddenly changed. On their first day on the Mattawa River, they awoke to the coldest weather yet. By afternoon, however, the wind shifted to the south. The men had their shirts off, and their backs were soon glistening in the sun.

That evening, as the brigade rounded a quick bend, Beloît spotted a deer swimming across the river. "Supper off the port bow," he sang out. The young doe saw the canoe bearing down and pumped her legs violently to escape.

Beloît aimed his pistol and fired. Pierre winced, but there was only a click. The men, starved for meat, let out a collective groan. Recalling Bellegarde's duck soup and trying to imagine how the cook might fit a deer into his kettle, Pierre secretly cheered for the animal to escape.

Beloît tossed his gun aside and grabbed a metal-shoed setting pole. He swung hard, catching the deer flush on the head. The animal went limp, and the men howled with joy.

Pierre shuddered when he heard the deer's skull crack. The violence stunned him. Here was a gentle, warm day at last, he thought, spoiled by sudden blood. It wasn't that he'd never seen a deer killed. Since he'd turned ten, he had hunted deer and rabbits and grouse with his father. Nearly everyone in Lachine depended on wild game, especially venison, to supplement their diets. But this rude killing—made worse, no doubt, by Beloît's hands—violated the peace of the day. To Pierre it was like witnessing a murder in a church.

The men were totally unbothered, and on shore a holiday atmosphere prevailed. Everyone whistled and sang as they gathered firewood. The only tense moment came when Bellegarde approached the deer carcass with his dirty knife and La Londe yelled, "Hands off."

"The cooking's my job," Bellegarde insisted.

Beloît added, "You tend your soup pot."

The cook withdrew, grumbling, and before the fire had even burned down to coals, Beloît and La Londe gutted, skinned, and quartered the deer. Soon the smell of roasting venison was overpowering the stale odor of boiled corn. The men looked ready to bite off a half-cooked hunk. Beloît teased them, saying, "This meat's for our canoe. You can do your own hunting."

La Petite said, "It's not funny to joke with starving men."

"Who's joking?" countered Beloît. "Nobody's ever starved on a diet of good boiled corn."

Despite the teasing, there was meat enough for everyone. After one tentative taste, Pierre tore into a juicy slab, not even noticing that he burned the roof of his mouth on the sizzling fat.

When he was finished, Pierre sat back and looked at the savage men around him. Emile's face was slick with grease, and his curly head was capless for a change. The back of Beloît's hands were still bloody from his butchering, but he sat, unbothered as always by his uncleanliness. The rest of the crew sat in the flickering firelight, grinning like wolves sated by a fresh kill.

La Londe stood up and patted his bulging stomach. "Looks like we have a little extra cargo to portage tomorrow, my friend."

Pierre smiled and wiped the grease from his own face with his shirt sleeve. Then he crawled toward the shelter of his canoe, anxious for the comfort of sleep.

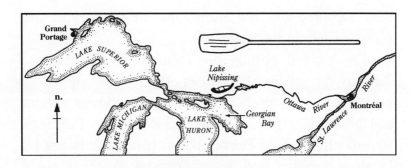

CHAPTER 11

◆

The French River

THE GOOD WEATHER held, and the spirits of the crew remained high as they paddled the length of the Mattawa. At Talon Falls, the point where their upstream labors ended, the *voyageurs* held an impromptu celebration. La Londe started things off by slipping the metal shoe off his setting pole. He needed to save the metal part for the trip back, but the wooden pole would not be needed on the big lakes ahead. Flinging it spear-fashion into the pool at the base of the falls, he yelled, "Goodbye, and good riddance to ugly upstream poling."

The crew cheered as the other bowmen tossed their poles aside too. The middlemen splashed each other with their paddles, and one overexuberant fellow knocked Pierre's cap into the water.

The rugged portage to Trout Lake did little to dampen the spirits of the men. Pierre was amazed at how fast they covered the interlinked series of creeks and beaver ponds that led to Lake Nipissing. The bugs were horrible. Once Pierre opened his mouth to ask La Londe a question, and he swallowed a cluster of gnats in a single gulp. La Londe laughed and slapped him on the back saying, "A little extra meat will do you good, my friend, but leave a few for seed. You don't want to eat up all the breeding stock."

As they began their traverse of Nipissing, the men feathered their paddles, turning them flat into the wind on each forward stroke and pulling at a quicker than normal pace without any urging.

"What's the hurry?" Pierre turned and asked Charbonneau.

"Nipissing is too shallow. Easy to be *dégradé*."

"The waves are worse on shallow lakes?" Pierre asked.

Charbonneau nodded. He was in no mood to chat. Pierre knew the meaning of *dégradé*. His father sometimes talked about being wind-bound on Superior and Huron, but the idea of being stuck on an inland lake was new to Pierre.

They took a pipe stop on an island near the middle of

the lake, and Pierre went for a walk. At the edge of a clearing only a dozen paces from the beach, Pierre was shocked to find three red crosses made from broken paddles and tied together with rawhide thongs.

"It's a sad sight, eh, Pierre?" Pierre was startled by La Londe, who was looking over his shoulder at the markers. "All that's left is a splash of red paint and a broken paddle blade. A sudden squall . . . a rock in the bow . . . and the cold does its trick." La Londe paused and ran his fingers through his famous hair. "Then the company writes a fancy letter."

Pierre knew about those letters. One afternoon when he was small, he was trying to sneak up on a pigeon in the barn loft with his slingshot. Camille, who was standing at the base of the ladder, yelled to scare the bird away. When he turned to shush his sister, Pierre saw a lone courier riding toward their cabin. "Mother," he called to the house, "a man's coming."

By the time Pierre climbed down, Mother was standing in the doorway, pale and tight-lipped. Pierre was confused, since strangers were always welcome at their home. Only after his mother gave the horseman directions to a house at the far end of the village did she explain that one of Father's *voyageur* friends had died.

"I've seen the letters they bring, Pierre," she said. "They come with money that means nothing, and they flower up dying with grand words like *pride* and *service* and *duty*. They speak of the 'good of the company.' But what it all comes down to is dead and drowned and never ever coming through that door again. . . ." Her voice trailed off as she stared in the direction of the vanishing man.

The next morning the energy of the men reached a new level when they broke camp and started down the French River. La Londe told Pierre the seventy-mile stretch of water that led to Lake Huron would be an easy one-day run. "It's a downhill ride all the way," he said. "We take a few light pulls, and the river she does the rest." Pierre was amazed at La Londe's enthusiasm. Though he was always positive, his face revealed a special energy this day.

Though La Londe exaggerated a bit—they did have to paddle at their normal rate—their speed was more than doubled by the swift current. When the brigade got to the first rapids, Pierre saw why his bowman was so excited to be on the French River.

McKay and La Petite climbed onto some boulders that gave them a clear downstream view. "The left-hand channel's clear all the way," La Petite called out over the roaring of the water.

"Get ready for the sleigh ride, gentlemen," La Londe said.

One by one the canoes rocketed down the white

chute. When it was Charbonneau's turn, he allowed for a safe spacing between his craft and the one ahead; then he yelled, "Pull!"

The paddles flashed triple-time. Speed was the key in running white water. If they didn't keep their craft going faster than the water racing beneath the hull, they were left to the whim of the current. Without proper speed the steersman had no control.

Just when the big Montréal was going faster than Pierre ever thought it could, they entered the rapids. La Londe twirled his paddle above his head and cut loose with a high-pitched yell. "Hang on, *hivernants!*" he hollered.

Time froze as the bow of the canoe jutted out over empty air. The four front paddlers held their blades a moment above the white spillway that fell suddenly out of reach. When the bow finally plunged down, the stern lurched skyward, nearly catapulting Pierre out of his seat. *"Eeeee . . . ,"* the boy screamed, and the men yelled and whistled, but the roar of the water drowned them out. A fine mist filled the air as La Londe's ghost-white hair blew straight back off his shoulders, and the hull hurtled down, down, down.

A minute later their quarter-mile run was done. As the grinning canoemen paddled across the pool below the rapids, Pierre's heart was still racing. The whole way down the rapids he'd thought of nothing but the red crosses that dotted the waterways behind them. Would they place one here for me, as young as I am? he wondered.

"So how was the ride, Pierre?" Charbonneau asked. If anyone had heard him scream, it was Charbonneau.

Gulping a deep breath to steady himself, Pierre replied, "It was better than a carry."

Charbonneau laughed. "Spoken like a true canoeman. At least we start you out gently."

"Gently?" Pierre tried to control his astonishment.

"*Gentle* is the word for this sault here," Charbonneau said, motioning with his head as he spoke. "It is straight and deep. That's the easy kind. Even in low water a man can run it blindfolded. But the shallow ones, and the ones with quick twists and turns—those are a dog of another color."

"Any tough rapids on the French?" Pierre tried to sound relaxed.

"This is mainly clean chutes. Some are a bit tight—we may scrape our gunwales now and then—but there's no tricky parts until we near the outlet. There we have a snaky patch of water that will take some good bow work." He paused. "Not scared, are you?"

"This old-timer? Scared?" Pierre scoffed, as Charbonneau laughed.

The closer they got to Lake Huron, the more the channel narrowed. Just when Pierre thought the river couldn't get any tighter, they shot into the yawning mouth of a gorge that quickly narrowed to only ten or twelve feet. Sheer rock walls rose up to block out the sun.

For a hundred yards they skimmed down this rock "gut," paddling as room allowed but mainly giving themselves over to the skill of the foreman's steering. Once their left gunwale scraped against the side and knocked loose a moss-covered chunk of rock. Another time La Londe had to rap his paddle hard against the cliff to keep the bow from veering too far off line. Pierre edged toward the middle of the canoe, his eyes wide and his mouth open.

When they finally shot out into the light, La Londe called, "Hold the right channel." The paddlers on the left dug hard.

Then Pierre saw one of the tricky turns that Charbonneau had mentioned. At a place where the river momentarily widened into a foaming pool, they had to make a quick right turn. Since their speed threatened to carry them straight ahead onto the rocks, the men on the left paddled with all their might. Those on the right obeyed La Londe's command: "Ship your oars," and they stopped paddling.

The bow veered faster to the right than anyone expected, and La Londe called, "Backwater left," but their abrupt right turn continued. The long canoe swung directly toward a foam-topped boulder. La Londe set his paddle against the rock.

Pierre heard a sharp crack as La Londe's paddle

snapped in two. "Backwater," the bowman yelled one more time as he bent to grab a spare blade.

Just then the bow bumped up onto the boulder and the stern began to swing around. Pierre heard a yell behind him. He turned to see McKay's canoe flying out of the chute above them, bearing straight for their canoe.

La Londe took a quick glance upriver, and then he tried one last, desperate shove against the submerged boulder. The muscles under his loose shirt quivered, but the bow wouldn't budge. The stern swung faster now in the current, and despite the frantic backpaddling of the crew, it looked as if they would be broadsided when McKay's canoe arrived.

"No," Charbonneau bellowed. Pierre closed his eyes, anticipating the shuddering crunch of a canoe shearing through their hull. When there was no impact, he opened his eyes just in time to see La Londe leap over the side. Still clinging to the gunwale, the bowman planted both feet on the slippery boulder, grabbed the projecting bow in his hands, and heaved upward.

As the front of the canoe came free, the fierce backpaddling of the middlemen finally took effect. The stern swung back just as McKay's canoe brushed past, cutting so close that it knocked a paddle out of one man's hand.

In that same instant La Londe lost his footing. Before anyone could extend a hand or even cry out, he was gone.

One moment he was there, and an instant later there was only the boulder and a white horsetail of water.

Pierre turned to Charbonneau and yelled, "A rope! Get a rope!" but everyone's eyes were already turned downstream, searching for a reason to hope.

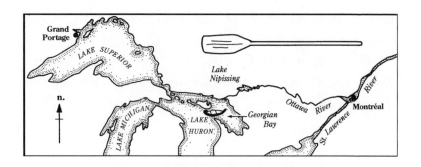

CHAPTER 12

A Broken Blade

BY THE TIME Charbonneau's canoe reached Lake Huron, Pierre could see that McKay had already ordered the search to begin. Three of the Montréals paddled back and forth across the outlet of the French River, while the crewmen scanned the water with hopeful eyes. A dozen men combed the shore of the lake, while a dozen others ran back up the river, hoping to find some trace of the missing man. A half hour later La Petite returned from his search upriver. He was holding the blade of La Londe's paddle.

They searched for an hour in silence. Just before sundown Charbonneau found the second half of La Londe's paddle floating well out into the lake. He scooped up the broken piece, declaring simply, "The big lakes don't like to give up their dead."

For a long while no one moved or spoke, and the canoe floated silently across the black water. Finally Emile spoke to no one in particular: "It's a cold, mean place to lie forever."

A few minutes later Charbonneau turned the boat toward shore. The cool, damp smell of night was already in the air. Pierre fought back his tears, remembering what Bellegarde said that first day on the beach about never feeling sorry "for no man what's still alive."

Pierre recalled the coffin they'd met at St. Anne's Chapel. He closed his eyes a moment and imagined the corpse of La Londe drifting in the cold current of Huron. His hair waved gently in green light, as his body, pale arms and legs extended, sank deeper into the darkness.

Later, as the men rolled out their blankets, there was none of the usual joking. Emile, who was preparing his bed nearby, looked toward Pierre just as he reached to untie his knife. Emile stared at the carved handle and asked, "Why did it have to be him?"

Pierre shook his head. He had seen the same question in every man's eyes tonight, and he suspected no one knew the answer. For now he didn't want to talk or think. Though he wasn't physically tired, he felt an incredible weariness, and he wanted to lie down.

"And look what we're stuck with," Emile continued,

tilting his head toward Jean Beloît. "That fellow's deserved drowning every day of his life, but he'll probably live to a hundred."

Pierre nodded. Feeling wicked, he almost smiled at the thought of Beloît drowning. If only that cackling fool had been silenced by the dark waters!

Though the next morning was warm and brilliant blue, the men moved as if they were numb with cold. In silence they paddled up and down the shore for an hour, dutifully trying one last time to find their bowman's body.

Then Pierre helped La Petite and Charbonneau tie La Londe's broken paddle together in the shape of a cross and paint it with vermilion dye borrowed from a parcel of trade goods. They hiked up the hill and set the cross in a pile of rocks next to a half dozen markers. La Petite and Charbonneau started back, but Pierre lingered a moment.

He looked to the east and suddenly hated the calm blueness of Huron. He picked up a rock and heaved it as far as he could. Before the first stone clattered onto the boulders that rimmed the French River gorge, he threw another and another. When Pierre finally stopped, he was panting hard. He wasn't sure how many stones he'd flung at the river, but the edge of his anger was blunted.

Before the brigade headed out, John McKay assembled the men on the beach and said a few words. McKay ran his hand through his bushy red beard and coughed once before he started. "In life," he began, "we knew

Charles La Londe as a loyal friend and a skilled canoeman. For the past two decades he was a dedicated servant to the North West Company. Even as we grieve we are grateful to him for his service and for his recent act of heroism, which saved an entire canoe from certain destruction. He is an example of courage and commitment to us all." McKay stopped a moment and looked at his men. Pierre bit his lip.

"It is hard for us to say goodbye," he continued, "to a man so kind and good." Pierre was impressed with the ministerlike tone in McKay's voice. "Yet lest we be tempted in our grief to question Providence, may I remind you of the Ninety-eighth Psalm." McKay paused to open a small brown Bible. "The Lord warns us to prepare, saying, 'What man is he that liveth and shall not see death?' "

McKay looked up at his men and continued. "Whether our parting from this world comes early or late, sudden or slow, it is not our place to question. We take up our journey without knowing where or when it will end. Each man in his turn must one day pass on to greater kingdoms.

"For as the prophet Job reminds us: 'The waters wear away the stones and wash away the things which grow out of the dust of the earth. Man that is born of woman is of few days and full of trouble. He cometh forth like a flower and is cut down. He fleeth also as a shadow and continueth not.' "

After a moment of silence, the commander concluded,

reciting as the men joined in: " 'The Lord is my Shepherd. I shall not want. He maketh me to lie down in green pastures. He leadeth me beside still waters . . .' "

The men stood a few minutes in silence before walking to their canoes. After they boarded their canoe, Charbonneau's crew paused to look up at the red marker. Each man doffed his cap and crossed himself before taking up his paddle. Then one by one the blades began their familiar dip and pull.

A hundred yards out, Pierre glanced back at the hill one last time. La Londe's newly painted marker made the old ones look shabby. His cross looked larger, too, catching more light than all the rest and casting a shadow back over the hill that looked like a huge arrow about to be released on a blurring, upstream flight.

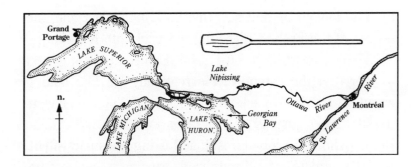

CHAPTER 13

La Cloche Rock

WHEN PIERRE WAS only eight his grandfather back in France had died. Since he had never met the man, he hadn't understood his mother's tears. Though Mother told him her father was "a wise man . . . tall and noble . . . a professor at the Sorbonne," to Pierre he remained a faceless shadow.

With La Londe it was the opposite situation. La Londe had been all too real. Awake or asleep—it made no difference—Pierre could see La Londe's face grinning above the gunwale as he lifted the canoe free, not knowing that only an instant later he would be dead. Without thinking, Pierre would listen for La Londe's singing; then every

97

time he looked up and saw that La Londe was gone, the horror of the French River flashed back into his mind.

Their second night on Huron, Emile was sitting next to Pierre at the campfire. Pierre finally felt like talking about La Londe. He asked his friend, "Do you ever wonder if there's justice?" Both boys were staring at Jean Beloît, who was off by himself and being unusually silent.

"It's hard to say," Emile said, pausing to pull off his cap and run his fingers through his tangled hair. "Maybe what seems unfair for now will even out in the end?"

"In other words," Pierre said, "if we're patient, one day certain disgusting idiots will get what they deserve, and then—"

Charbonneau overheard the boys and interrupted. Pierre braced himself for a lecture. The steersman would tell them to toughen up and get on with their lives. Instead, his voice was soft rather than soldierly. "There's nothing harder to accept than a good man dying young. Calling it fate or the will of God or bad luck doesn't help, either." He paused with his steely eyes reflecting bits of embers from the fire. "Everyone of us is just as angry as you young fellows, but the years have a way of numbing a man. We've all seen it happen so many times that a part of us has died with every mate that went down. We care, but we can't let the sadness touch us too deep. A good man is gone, but if we lose our edge, the lake will be burying us all."

When Charbonneau walked off, Pierre stared after

him with new respect. There was clearly more to this man than the tough face he showed to the world.

The north shore of Lake Huron was two hundred miles of spectacular canoeing. With no portages to slow them down, and with a string of islands to protect them from onshore winds, the brigade made great time.

The days were clear and warm, and Pierre paddled without his shirt or cap. When he went bareheaded the old timers teased him about being "out of uniform," but after the chilly days on the Ottawa, Pierre enjoyed the feel of the sun. Like his father, he tanned quickly, and like his sisters', his hair bleached to an almost white blond. The muscles in his arms and shoulders began to stand out as a result of his thousands of paddle strokes. But with La Londe gone from his place in the bow, the beauty of the days was empty for Pierre.

On the third consecutive day of clear skies, Pierre was surprised when Charbonneau started complaining. "I don't like the look of this. It's all wrong. This isn't what Huron's supposed to be in June."

"Don't be such a doomsayer," Emile declared with a grin.

"We'll pay for this later," Charbonneau insisted. "We'll be begging this weather back. I tell you, it's not normal."

"Enjoy it while you can," Beloît chided him.

Charbonneau waved a hand at the islands. "I've seen good weather wasted on Huron before. We can take anything here. It's on Superior we'll be wanting the help. That lake is two hundred fathoms in places and so cold she makes a climate all her own. It might be summer up on those hills, but here on the water, a squall can bring it down to freezing in minutes."

The crew bullied their steersman into silence with a chorus of boos, but his comments made Pierre nervous. Father called Superior the Big Lake, and he often spoke of its wild spring storms. Pierre also knew that La Londe's death weighed heavily on everyone. *Voyageurs* liked to pretend they would never die, but the bowman's tragic end served notice to everyone.

For Charbonneau's crew, La Londe's absence was even harder. Their newly appointed bowman was Beloît. While La Londe had urged the men on with his songs and positive encouragement, Beloît was like a snarling dog.

"Paddle, ladies," he'd yell at the crew. "You pull like a bunch of old hags. Is it time for the rocking chairs?"

He saved his best insults for Pierre, calling him whatever came to mind: puppy, whelp, snail, baby. It made no difference that his strokes were getting quick and clean. Pierre knew it was selfish, but when the name-calling was at its worst, he almost felt angry at La Londe for dying and leaving him with Beloît.

Though he'd dreaded taking on full days of paddling, Pierre discovered that the open water was small work compared to the Ottawa. The portages and the miles of upstream paddling had toughened both his body and his mind. He could paddle for hours at a time now, free from the effort of thought.

"How many strokes so far today, Pierre?" Charbonneau teased him.

"How many strokes?" Pierre echoed, remembering his former clumsy self. Those first few days of the trip he'd shared his counting with no one. "Who says I count strokes?"

"You did, but you don't, right?" Charbonneau laughed. "It was that way with us all. At first you count every paddle stroke and mark every mile, then soon you are too tired to do anything but forget. The work comes easier, and most important of all"—he chuckled—"the rest of us stay dry." Pierre was surprised at Charbonneau's gentle humor, and he was proud that the steersman had noticed the improvement in his paddling.

The weather stayed perfect as they worked their way along Huron's shore. To the north, bare, quartz-flecked hills rose up from the water's edge. To the south, beyond the offshore islands, Huron stretched off in open blue.

One day, while they were navigating through a strait barely wide enough for the canoes, they passed a magical boulder called La Cloche. In anticipation of this event Beloît had scavenged a rock during their last pipe stop.

"Listen to the bell, schoolboy," Beloît said, turning and waving to Pierre as they approached the huge rock.

Pierre wished they could maroon this fool on the boulder. He would die a slow death as he deserved, and the seagulls would peck out his dirty black eyes.

The men shipped their paddles, and the canoe went into a silent glide. Beloît leaned over and rapped the gigantic basalt boulder with the rock in his fist. A deep, mournful tolling issued from the very core of the stone, startling Pierre. It sounded like a bell within a bell. He'd never heard anything to match the depth of its tone. Every crewman listened in silence as the note echoed like a chord struck in an earth-locked cavern.

Pierre was still enjoying the beauty of the moment when Beloît started his infernal cackling. "Pretty music, ain't it?" he crowed. "I swear, it's as sweet as a church choir—"

"Church choir?" Charbonneau interrupted. "Just what would you know about a church or a choir?"

"Ha!" Beloît laughed. "That's a good one. Ha! Ha! Ha!"

Pierre pulled again on his paddle, glad to work at forgetting evil men and nicknames and deaths that shouldn't be.

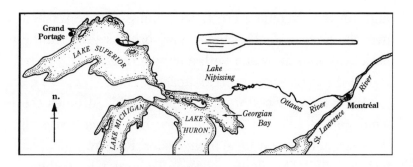

CHAPTER 14

Huron's Revenge

THE FINE WEATHER held for their traverse of Huron and a
two-day layover in Sault Sainte Marie. Their first full day
on Lake Superior was perfect as well. Then, after breaking camp on the second morning, the brigade decided to
save twenty miles by cutting straight across a huge bay
called Michipicoten. As usual, the crew teased Charbonneau about his dire predictions. Beloît wet his finger and
tested the breeze. "Can this be the curse of Huron fallen
upon us, Charbonneau?" he asked. Everyone laughed.

Thirty minutes later no one was joking. Huge white-
caps rolled out of the west. The bow slid like the nose of a
great sea beast down the backside of each wave and rose

high on the oncoming crest. Sometimes a wave washed over the prow, and other times a big breaker dropped the bark hull onto the water with a shuddering crack. Pierre feared the canoe would break apart.

His hands burned from the biting cold. At times the wind gusted so hard that the crew had to pull with all their strength to stay dead in the water. Raindrops popped into the hull like flung pebbles. To forget his aching, Pierre thought of home. He tried to recall happy times, such as the spring day when he and Camille and Celeste had sailed little hand-carved boats on the creek behind their house, and a wagon trip he and his family had taken to Montréal on Bastille Day when he was ten, but his mind kept drawing back to a single dark image from just a summer ago.

That afternoon Pierre was swimming with his friends down at the company landing. He was surfacing near the pier when an older boy pushed him under as a joke. At first Pierre thought nothing of it. Even when the boy put his feet on Pierre's back and pressed him down to the bottom, he expected him to let go. Then, as Pierre listened to the muffled laughter from above, he was suddenly afraid. The boy wouldn't get off. He tried to lift him, but the dim laughter continued. Pierre's head pounded. Waves of red and black swept through his brain. Just before he was ready to swallow a huge gulp of water, he dug his fingernails into the boy's ankle, and the pressure was released.

When he broke the surface and spit out a mouthful of brown river water, his friends pointed and laughed.

Pierre played along with the joke. He smiled as he clutched the dock post and caught his breath. But even after his pulse returned to normal, he was still trembling inside.

As Pierre dug his paddle into the waves, he wondered how many minutes he could last in the icy waters of Superior if they swamped. If it was true what they said about the big lakes not giving up their dead, how long would it take for his body to sink twelve hundred feet?

Pierre was picturing the cold lips of a fish picking at his eyeballs when a shout from the front of the canoe shocked him back to the present. It was Beloît. "Hold on," the bowman yelled.

Beloît stood with his thighs braced against the gunwales. A cascade of water hit him full in the chest, but he held his footing. Yelling like a warrior, the bowman reached with his paddle and pulled the canoe straight into the next swell.

In the brief calm that followed, Beloît turned to the rear of the canoe. "The kettle, Pierre," he shouted. It was his duty as the youngest crewman. Pierre bailed while the rest of the men paddled with all their strength.

The waves were getting higher now that the wind had the full force of four hundred miles of open lake behind it. And what was worse, the brigade had to angle across the waves to hold their course for the headland. Charbonneau steered as direct a route as he dared, knowing that the strength of his crew wouldn't allow a more gradual approach.

Beloît paid careful attention to each wave, shouting "Ship oars" when he wanted the bow to rise with a dangerous swell and yelling "Fall to" when he wanted the paddling to resume.

Quartering into the waves was becoming more dangerous, and turning around and running with the wind to the eastern shore would be suicide. Turning to Charbonneau, Beloît pointed with his paddle. "How about the island?" he shouted through the wind.

There was no answer. Pierre turned. Charbonneau was studying the big island. Shrouded in mist, it was only slightly closer than the headland of Michipicoten Bay. The clear advantage would be a direct upwind course.

"What do you say?" Beloît called again.

Charbonneau stared at the island, and then at the north shore of the bay. Emile and several other crewmen turned now, but no one spoke. There would be no survivors if they swamped.

Finally Charbonneau nodded. "Signal McKay!"

All five canoes turned upwind and headed straight for Michipicoten Island. They were no longer in danger of broaching, but they still had to struggle against the waves.

Emile offered to take a turn with the kettle, while

Pierre paddled again. Numb with cold and fatigue, Pierre's mind floated back to his church in Lachine. The candles were lit. The altar cloth and flowers were in place. Yet the only people in sight were Pierre and Celeste. Wearing a blue lace dress, she was standing in front where the priest should be. Her hair was tied back with white ribbons, and she smiled at Pierre. Just then the door opened and Father Michel, dressed in his Sunday robe, ran up the aisle, hurrying like a small boy who was late for school. Celeste's face darkened. The priest turned, and Pierre was shocked to see it was not the priest but the town doctor. He held out a huge pair of silver shears toward Celeste. Pinched between the tip of the bright blades was Pierre's father's severed thumb.

Pierre lurched forward. Ignoring the command to ship oars, he'd taken a paddle stroke in empty air.

"Whoa!" Charbonneau exclaimed, reaching with his paddle to keep Pierre from pitching sideways out of the canoe. "Stay in the saddle, son."

Just then there was a sickening crack amidships, as the canoe was caught on double crests and lifted both bow and stern. Had the seams split? Despite the bailing, the water in the canoe was now rising over the top of Pierre's moccasins.

An hour of paddling finally brought them into partial calm. The rain stopped, too, as they neared the island, but by now three men had to bail. With fewer men paddling, the water poured in even faster.

Pierre saw that the other canoes had reached shore, but they were still a quarter of a mile out. Must we die so close to a lee shore? he thought.

Beloît wrested another kettle from a pack and set one more man to bailing. They worked furiously, but the gunwales sank ever closer to the surface of the water.

La Petite could see their plight from shore and hastily unloaded his cargo. Recruiting four of his men, they soon paddled out to help.

Holding the canoes side by side, Charbonneau's crew used the last of their strength to transfer the freight from the foundering canoe. Even before the parcels were unloaded, the teasing began.

La Petite looked at the sorry fellows sitting calf-deep in chilly water and chuckled. "You know, gentlemen," he declared, "it works better to paddle over the lake instead of in it."

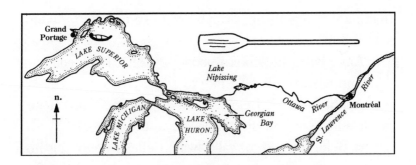

CHAPTER 15

Dégradé

THE SUN REAPPEARED the next morning, but the wind blew with such fury that the brigade was forced to stay on the island another day. For the first time they were what the canoemen called with great loathing *dégradé*.

For two days there was work enough to keep them busy. They dried out the freight and regummed their canoes, but by the third day of wind, Pierre noticed that any comment could start a quarrel.

When Bellegarde was serving his "soup" that night, the inevitable finally happened. Beloît grumbled as usual about the food. Though Bellegarde normally ignored him, that night he spoke up. "Maybe you like to cook for yourself, Beloît?"

"Any idiot could cook this slop," Beloît retorted.

"You are one idiot I'd like to see try."

"Achhh . . . ," Beloît hacked, spitting into Bellegarde's ladle and tossing his plate to the ground.

As Beloît turned to walk away, Bellegarde swung his metal scoop and caught the bowman on the side of the head. "Pig!" the cook yelled, as Beloît's cap flew off and corn and steaming liquid splattered everywhere.

With a roar Beloît charged into the older man, knocking him backward and pinning his arms to the ground with his knees. When Beloît cocked his fist, Pierre assumed it would end quickly. But Bellegarde thought fast. Arching his back with all his strength, he turned his head to one side and launched his knee upward.

Beloît groaned as Bellegarde's bony kneecap caught him in the groin, and at the same time, his fist missed Bellegarde's chin and hit the ground with a sickening crunch. For the next few minutes there was a flurry of punching.

The men yelled for Bellegarde to "Knock his block off!" or "Smash him good!" Emile and Pierre both jumped up and down, calling encouragement to the cook. Pierre clenched his fist and punched the air, wishing he could smack Beloît for every insult he'd hurled Pierre's way. Out of the corner of his eye, Pierre even saw that McKay was urging on old Bellegarde.

In spite of all the cheering, Beloît soon emerged on top. It would have ended there if he'd struck a fair blow. Instead, Beloît grabbed Bellegarde by both ears and pounded his head against the ground. La Petite decided this was more than Bellegarde deserved, so he bent down to pull Beloît off.

"He's had enough now, Jean," La Petite said.

But Beloît wasn't through. To everyone's amazement, Beloît, acting as if he'd gone crazy, jumped up and assaulted La Petite.

La Petite was taken off guard and fell to his knees. Then, to Pierre's horror, Beloît grabbed a stick of firewood from the pile by the soup kettle and took a swing at La Petite. Traveling with the full force of Beloît's paddle-toughened arms, the inch-wide piece of driftwood hit La Petite's head and splintered in half.

Emile yelled, "No!" and Charbonneau and Bellegarde both stepped forward to restrain Beloît. But before they could act, Beloît unleashed a kick at La Petite's stomach. Pierre lowered his head, sure that the kick would put La Petite down for good.

But when he heard a leathery *thwack,* instead of the thud of a blow he expected, Pierre looked up. La Petite caught Beloît's moccasin in his right hand and lifted his foot straight up. Beloît's shoulders slammed to the ground, with the sound of a beef slab hitting a butcher block. A rush of breath escaped Beloît, but the strength of his rage brought him to his feet.

Beloît lowered his head to charge, but this time La Petite was ready. Pierre saw one fist flash out, and an instant later the attacker was lying unconscious at the base of a pine tree.

Pierre guessed the men would talk for many years about what La Petite did next. Hurrying forward, the big man touched Beloît gently on the side of his neck and then bent to check his breathing.

After he was satisfied that Beloît was uninjured, La Petite called, "A kettle, Pierre." The men applauded when La Petite dumped the lake water over Beloît's head.

Beloît shook the confusion from his head and extended his hand. "Well struck, little fellow," he teased.

La Petite shook Beloît's hand then, laughing at this crazy idiot who had seemed so intent on killing him only moments before. Still chuckling, he said, "You do swing a mean stick, Jean. It's just like a bowman to mix his work and his pleasure."

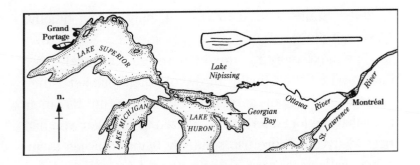

CHAPTER 16

◆

Prettying Up

To PIERRE'S SURPRISE the fight lifted the gloom of the brigade, and once they got back under way, they covered two hundred miles in only three days. Taking advantage of favorable winds, they hoisted their oilcloth tarps and sailed with little help from the paddles. "Bless *La Vieille*, the old lady of the wind," Charbonneau declared.

Their final afternoon on Superior they camped only ten miles from Grand Portage. Pierre asked Charbonneau, "Why don't we just paddle down to the fort tonight?" Though the steersman had been friendly lately, he dismissed this question without a reply, turning instead to prepare his bed.

Even Emile refused to explain, only saying quietly, "Just wait and see."

The next morning the men rested until well after dawn. When they finally threw off their blankets, they immediately began sprucing themselves up for their arrival at the fort. Pierre was amazed to see men who had been dirty the entire trip suddenly begin to preen themselves with great care. Some bathed. Some washed and combed their hair. The most conscientious in the group even unsheathed their hunting knives and trimmed their beards. The men pulled bright sashes and *capots* out of their packs and donned them with the deliberation of priests dressing in vestments.

Beloît hadn't ventured to rinse out so much as a handkerchief on any of their Sunday rest stops, yet he declared this morning his wash day. Before the sun was even full in the sky, the crude fellow stripped off his clothes and waded into the lake. He thrashed his shirts and pants and handkerchiefs around in the icy water, gave them a hasty wringing out, and spread them on the rocks to dry. Except for the dirty cap, which remained perched on his head, Beloît ate breakfast naked. No one seemed to notice or care. Only Mr. McKay bothered to joke, "Trying out a new summer uniform, Jean?"

Once breakfast was over, the men still showed no sign of leaving, so Pierre decided to go for a swim. He walked over to a rock ledge that had a deep drop-off. Peeling off his clothes, Pierre took a short run and leaped feetfirst into Superior. The cold stopped his breath, but Emile and Larocque, who were standing nearby, cheered his performance. Pierre climbed out, chilled to the bone but refreshed.

They left at midmorning, and it felt good to be back in the canoe and paddling at a stroke-a-second pace. Beloît took up a *chanson* and the others, out of pity for his croaky voice, joined in.

When they rounded Hat Point, Pierre finally saw the fort. He couldn't believe how simple the rude stockade was. Grand Portage was better known in the banking houses and royal courts of Europe than any other place in the Northwest Territory. His father spoke so reverently of the fort that Pierre had imagined a castle. Yet here it was, a lot of pointed logs stuck in the ground with wigwams and tents scattered around it.

Grand Portage was home to a thousand Ojibwa Indians who built canoes and supplied meat for the company. He also knew it was the rendezvous point for every trader headed west, yet the place looked deserted. There were only a handful of men between the stockade and the beach.

Just then La Petite called to Charbonneau. "How about a race to see who unloads?" Pierre groaned. He was sick of the teasing and sick of having to do everyone's work when they lost. He hadn't counted the races they'd lost to campsites and carrying places, but he thought there must have been hundreds. Pierre knew his crew's losses were his fault, and he was convinced a stronger paddler would have surely made a difference.

"Fall to," La Petite yelled.

Shouts went up from the canoes, and the men onshore began calling out encouragement. Three canoes pulled ahead, but Charbonneau's craft held the fourth position until they were only a hundred yards offshore. Then just when Pierre decided they had a chance, the trailing canoe surged past. Knowing they'd lost, Charbonneau's crew shipped their paddles and coasted to shore.

As they unloaded the freight, Beloît, who was unused to losing canoe races, complained to Charbonneau. "I don't like the idea of having to carry all these packs just because you got a bunch of milksops in your crew." Beloît leered at Pierre to lend emphasis to his words.

"Stop whining, Beloît," Charbonneau countered. "You had a paddle in your hand, too."

But Beloît wouldn't quit. "It takes more than one real man to handle a Montréal," he insisted. As he walked over to pick up his first parcel, he jabbed his elbow into Pierre's ribs and bumped him out of the way. Pierre nearly fell, but no one said a word.

Feeling totally alone, Pierre picked up a pack and started up the path to the storehouse. Even Emile avoided his eyes. Most of the men trotted as fast as they could up the hill, anxious to get the job done, but Pierre dragged behind. He was convinced his paddling had lost them the race. He thought everyone must be sick of him by now.

To make matters worse, each time Beloît met Pierre going up or down the path, the dark man insulted him. "If that pack's too heavy for you, *madame,*" he said one time, "I can get you a hatbox to carry." Another time Beloît said, "Perhaps we can find you a cane if the hill's too steep."

Pierre studied the stockade. He couldn't believe he'd traveled twelve hundred miles to find a row of log pickets stuck in the mud. For the first time since La Londe's death, Pierre felt like crying. He returned to the shore and picked up another parcel. Beloît, who had a full load on his back, noticed that his eyes were red. "What's the matter?" he chortled. "Crying for your mama?"

Ignoring the man, Pierre turned to hurry back up the trail, but Beloît stuck out his foot. Pierre sprawled across the path, and his pack ripped open. A stack of nested kettles fell clanging onto the rocks.

Beloît opened his mouth wide and guffawed. "You dropped your pot, Mother. How will you ever cook supper?"

Seized by a sudden rage, Pierre stood and swung his fist at Beloît. "My name is Pierre," he yelled, punching Beloît square in the stomach. The blow knocked the wind out of the bowman. He stumbled and lost his footing on the slippery rocks. Then, with his arms wheeling wildly, he pitched backward into the lake.

"*Ahhhhhh . . . ,*" Beloît bellowed. A column of water flew up, and the men began to laugh.

117

Beloît's feet were still on the shore, but the weight of his packs pulled his chest half underwater. He splashed his arms. "Help me, you idiots. Help."

"Lie still and we'll try," Charbonneau offered, stepping forward. "You might consider a please, too," Emile added.

Beloît bellowed, "Idiots!" but calmed himself when he almost tipped over onto his face. When Charbonneau and Emile finally pulled him out of the water, he shed his soggy pack and walked straight for Pierre.

Pierre felt like bolting for the fort, but he held his ground. With a weird grin, Beloît flexed his fingers. Pierre imagined a huge, knobby fist flashing toward him. Beloît grabbed Pierre's right hand and pried it open. "Just checking to see if you have a musket ball hidden there. You pack quite a wallop in that fist, Pierre."

Then there was more laughter, and the hauling was suddenly easier to bear. Pierre grabbed the nearest parcel, grateful to have escaped with his life, and proud that, even though it had taken six weeks of hard paddling, Beloît had finally called him by his rightful name.

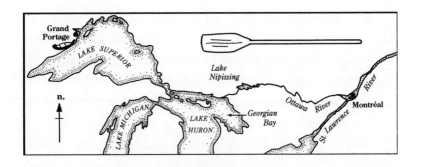

CHAPTER 17

Grand Portage

By the time Charbonneau's crew finished unloading, the rest of the brigade had tapped a brandy keg. "If you don't care to pickle your brain," Charbonneau offered, "I'll show you the grounds."

They walked beyond the stockade to the encampment. Pierre was surprised to see two separate camps with a rushing creek between them. One was for the pork eaters, the men who headed back to Montréal before autumn; the other was for the *hivernants,* the men who wintered in company outposts to the north.

"Why two camps? Don't they talk to each other?" Pierre asked.

Charbonneau laughed. Pierre was amazed at how relaxed the man was this afternoon. "They talk just fine," he answered. "The problem is their talk always leads to fighting. *Hivernants* like to boast, and the worst of the whole lot are the Athabascans. The company keeps 'em apart so they won't kill each other."

Pierre nodded. His father had told him many stories about Athabascans, that company of *voyageurs* who were legendary for their strength and endurance. Their standard packs were 110 pounds, and they were hired for five-year terms. They bragged constantly and liked to prove their toughness in fights with other *voyageurs.*

Up the hill behind the fort, Charbonneau stopped and announced grandly, "Here it is, the carry that everyone talks about—the Grand Portage itself." Pierre looked up the nearly vertical path. "One day," Charbonneau continued, "you'll be proud to tell your grandchildren you stood here. Fort Charlotte and the Pigeon River are nine miles off, but what makes the trip so brutal isn't the distance. There's a three-hundred-foot rise between here and there. The company tried horses and mules, but they decided it was cheaper to make men lame."

Pierre imagined the agony of such a carry and was glad to be a mere pork eater. The toughest portage on the Ottawa was nothing compared to this. The *hivernants* had good reason to brag.

Charbonneau led Pierre toward a maze of birch bark wigwams. "Let me introduce you to a few of my friends," he said, grinning like a man who'd been too long absent from home.

As they approached the edge of the Indian encampment, two men were wedging a long sheet of sewn birch bark between two rows of stakes that followed the rough outline of a north canoe. One of the men nodded to Charbonneau, but both kept working. Stones were piled on top of the bark sheeting to help form the hull. The men were getting ready to lash the gunwales to the top of the bark with cedar root lacing. "Next they'll fix the ribs in place," Charbonneau explained, "and then the thwarts and seats."

"That's all there is to it?" Pierre asked.

"Just a few days drying and she'll be ready to caulk."

Pierre looked at the graceful lines of the hull. He guessed the finished craft would be around twenty-five feet long. "Are the north canoes faster than a Montréal?" Pierre asked.

"Not only faster, but easier to portage and maneuver. The Ojibwa have been perfecting these boats for centuries. You can run white water that would stave in a lake canoe." Charbonneau was tracing the curve of the hull as he spoke. "Why, I remember one day when we were running the Namakan River . . ."

Suddenly there was a war whoop behind them. Pierre whirled to see a tall Indian smothering Charbonneau in his arms. At first Pierre thought his companion was being attacked, but then he saw Charbonneau grin. As he squeezed Charbonneau tight, the Indian sang out, "Charbonneau, you old bone shaker."

They pushed each other back to arms' length, and Charbonneau had a chance to speak. "So how was your winter, Mukwa?"

Pierre had never seen anything like Mukwa. To keep from laughing, Pierre covered his open mouth with his hand. The brave wore a wide-brimmed hat with a sash wrapped around the crown, holding three ostrich feathers high above his head. A silk handkerchief was tied at his throat, and a red checkered shirt showed beneath his blue waistcoat. Lace was pinned to the shoulders and sleeves of the coat, and he wore dark burgundy knee breeches. Though he didn't wear shoes, Pierre noticed a gray sock on one foot and a red one on the other, each held up by a silk garter.

"You know the winters, my friend," Mukwa replied. "The game goes a little farther out each year, but we survive." The Indian spoke excellent French. He grabbed Charbonneau by the shoulders again. "It is good to see you, Charbonneau."

They squatted on the ground and visited awhile longer, sharing news of the past year. After Charbonneau explained La Londe's death, he said, "We better get back to the fort and report in."

"I understand," Mukwa said. "But you must promise to feast with us before you leave this place."

"I'd be flattered."

"We will talk of old times," he said, "and bring your little friend. He can meet my daughter, Kennewah. Now off with you."

As soon as they were out of earshot, Pierre showed his anger at being called a "little friend." "Where did he ever get an outfit like that one?" he sneered.

"He's the chief, and he wears what he wants."

"A chief called Mukwa?"

"*Mukwa* means 'bear' in Ojibwa," Charbonneau explained patiently. "The bear is a powerful spirit. As a member of the Bear Clan, he could tell you many stories, but according to custom, winter is the only season to share the old legends." He stopped. Since La Londe's death, Charbonneau's gruff, military manner had softened, and Pierre appreciated the way he often went out of his way to explain things.

"But I always thought Indian chiefs wore headdresses and buffalo robes," Pierre said.

"Mukwa wears what his people regard as the finest dress of the civilized world. Bright clothes are a sign of wealth. The traders encourage it, too—they're always willing to swap a bit of lace or a handkerchief for pelts. So the chief gets a bit gaudier every year."

"Do all the chiefs dress like that?"

"No." Charbonneau chuckled as he replied. "Though you do run into a showy fellow now and then, farther inland the Indians dress as they always have. The men wear breechclouts, beaded leggings, and moccasins. The women . . ." He paused for the slightest moment. "The women wear the softest doeskin shifts you could ever imagine. They're all decorated with tiny beads and colored grasses and quills. In winter they wear rabbit-skin robes."

Charbonneau looked at Pierre's intent face. "We'd better check in with McKay before he decides we've run off to parts unknown."

As they made their way back down the rocky hillside, Pierre tried to picture an inland village such as Charbonneau described. The dark-eyed women in their beaded doeskin dresses sounded like perfect visions from a dream.

As they neared the stockade, Pierre saw that Grand Portage had come alive. Though only two dozen men had greeted them that morning, there seemed to be a thousand people milling around the stockade now. Charbonneau scoffed, "Looks like the rascals have crawled out of bed. All it takes is the scent of rum to roust them out."

That night a magnificent banquet was held in the great hall. Traders, clerks, and interpreters crowded along plank tables heaped with honey-glazed ham, venison, smoked trout, bread and butter, peas, Indian corn, potatoes, and fresh milk. Mr. McKay and the other North West Company officials sat at a head table, but except for some fancy bottles of wine, their fare was no better than that of the men from the brigades.

Six weeks of corn and salt pork had left Pierre ravenous for real food. Of all the elegant dishes placed before him, he savored the garden peas and milk most of all. He'd scorned vegetables back home, but the sweet, buttery flavor of the fresh-picked peas stirred his senses to a level of delight only surpassed by the thick, cream-topped mugs of milk. When his belly was full, Pierre sat back, a picture of contentment. From across the table, Emile gave him a broad grin and said, "Do you suppose we could get Bellegarde to stop by the kitchen for lessons?"

"They'd throw him out on his ear," Pierre said, chuckling.

"Or at least make him take a bath first," Emile added.

As soon as the meal was over, Pierre was surprised to see the men carry the tables to the far end of the room. A bagpipe, fiddle, and flute appeared; and just as the music started, some young Indian women showed up at the door. Dressed in their Sunday best, the men picked out partners and bowed.

Beloît, being slower than his mates to notice the women, nearly trampled two fellows en route to the door. Displaying a cavalier spirit, he dropped to one knee before the lady of his liking.

Pierre watched with pity, imagining the horror that would fill the girl's eyes when Beloît lifted his scarred face.

"Watch this," Pierre whispered to Charbonneau. "That girl will scream for sure when she sees his ugly mug."

To Pierre's surprise, the pretty girl smiled and nudged the friend beside her. When Beloît offered his arm, he and his chosen promenaded proudly to the dance floor.

"Did you see that?" Pierre was shocked.

"What? Beloît and the girl?"

"Yes. She's so pretty and he's . . ."

"An awful mess," Charbonneau offered, chuckling at Pierre's astonishment. "It's a different world up here. Scars are a fact of life in the wilderness. They're badges of honor—tokens of a life lived hard and well."

Pierre was still shaking his head in disbelief when he felt someone tap his shoulder. He turned to see a pretty Indian girl standing beside him. When she said something in Ojibwa to Pierre, Charbonneau burst out laughing.

"What did she say?" Pierre asked, embarrassed by the sudden attention.

"She says she wants to dance with the handsome young Frenchman," Charbonneau translated. "Apparently all the young girls are talking about you. They like your blond hair and your big muscles."

"I thought you were an honest steersman," Pierre said.

"That's what the lady said."

"Are you serious?"

"Believe what you want," Charbonneau replied, "but be polite. She's waiting for an answer?"

"Ah . . ." Pierre was flustered. "Tell her that I don't know how to dance."

Charbonneau grinned. He turned to the girl and spoke.

When he finished, she took Pierre's hand and led him onto the floor. Pierre glared back at Charbonneau, who grinned innocently. "Don't look at me," he said. "I only told her that you love dancing even more than paddling your canoe." He laughed then as Pierre disappeared among the whirling men and women.

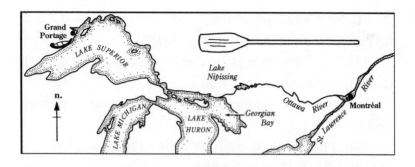

Grand Portage

LAKE SUPERIOR

Lake Nipissing

n.

LAKE MICHIGAN

LAKE HURON

Georgian Bay

Ottawa River

St. Lawrence River

Montréal

CHAPTER 18

◆

Mukwa's Wigwam

"How long will we be staying at the fort?" Pierre asked Charbonneau the next morning.

After complaining about "too many questions before breakfast," Charbonneau explained that their layover would last a week. He told Pierre the crew would reassemble, less McKay and several others who were taking the trade goods north. The Montréal canoes would bring baled furs back to Lachine, while the north canoes headed into the wilderness.

During his vacation from paddling, Pierre wandered through the fort and encampments. Though he ran an occasional errand for Charbonneau or La Petite, he had a lot of free time. Mainly he listened to the old-timers and learned as much as he could about the century-old trading system of the Northwest Territory.

One afternoon Pierre was helping La Petite sort through a load of trade goods. The big fellow tossed him one of the famous North West trading muskets to put on the gun rack. "Be careful," La Petite cautioned. "You're holding twenty plus in your hands."

Pierre looked at the brass side plate of the gun with its familiar etched dragon and shook his head. "How can you keep track of all those pluses?"

"Why, it's simple, lad," McKay answered. "They're trading credits. One plus equals one prime beaver pelt. All our company men use the same formula. As each season begins, they give the Indian trappers credits based on the value of a prime beaver pelt. A butcher knife is worth one plus, a woolen blanket eight, a North West gun twenty, and other things like kettles, hatchets, ironworks, cloth, and needles all have their own values."

"You give the Indians trade goods before they even bring in furs?"

"Aye," McKay responded. "It's all based on trust. I've seen some cheating done, but the whites mainly author it. If you give an Ojibwa a rifle in the fall, you can count on twenty pelts come spring."

"But what about other furs?" Pierre asked.

"If a prime beaver hide is one plus, a silver fox or a good bear hide can be worth three or even four plus.

Some are worth a lot less. It might take eight muskrat hides to equal a single plus. It all depends. Even the grade of beaver can vary. The finest we call winter-greased beaver. It's caught in cold weather when the pelt is prime. Then it's worn by the Indians until the long hairs fall out, leaving it velvet soft. Why so much interest in the trade?" McKay inquired. "Are ye thinking of wintering with us some season?"

"Me? In an outpost?" Pierre reddened at the thought of becoming an *hivernant*.

"Aye. And if you don't like the bull work, tend to your studies—we need a lot of smart fellows to keep track of the money that pours in and out of the frontier."

McKay turned away. Pierre felt proud that his commander thought him smart enough to work as a clerk someday. When he considered the weight of a quill pen compared to a paddle, maybe schooling made sense after all.

The trade item that McKay didn't mention was the one that caused the most trouble: rum. On only his second afternoon at the fort, Pierre watched as two fellows who'd been drinking got into an argument over a woman just outside the stockade. It looked like an innocent squabble until one of the men pulled out a knife and jabbed it into his rival's kneecap. The wounded man stabbed the other fellow twice in the chest.

The speed of it was dumbfounding. The braves were

standing in the sun talking, and an instant later one was bleeding to death in the dust. With the help of his friends, the man with the gashed knee limped home, while the other was carried to the dispensary to die.

Later that day, the brother of the dead man, a boy of only ten, went to the house of the man who'd killed his brother. He pushed the muzzle of a North West gun through the doorway and pulled the trigger.

There were two funerals the next day. Pierre got a glimpse of one of them when he and Charbonneau were walking to Mukwa's for dinner. Charbonneau paused in front of a crowded wigwam.

Through the doorway Pierre saw a number of Ojibwa, both male and female, clustered around the corpse. They were drinking and crying. One man sat at the feet of the corpse, staring into space, while a woman knelt at the head of the body and sobbed, pouring liquor down the dead man's throat.

"What are they doing?" Pierre whispered.

"I'm not sure." Charbonneau shook his head. "Maybe they think the dead are just as fond of rum as the living."

They walked on. Pierre asked how he'd met Mukwa.

Charbonneau chuckled. "That's a strange one. I found him one winter near an outpost up on Lake Vermilion about nineteen or twenty years back." Charbonneau paused. "He was just a boy, lying half dead in the snow. A Sioux war party had killed his entire family. Though

Mukwa had a musket ball in his shoulder and another in his leg, he crawled across some thin creek ice and escaped. I built a fire to thaw him out and hauled him home on my dogsled. After I dug the lead out with a skinning knife, I waited for him to die, but he toughed it out. Following the custom of his people, he's been forever grateful."

When they arrived at Mukwa's wigwam, Pierre was impressed by the quiet order. His wife, three children, and aged mother all greeted the visitors with polite nods, but they left the talking to the chief.

The meal was superb. The courses included roast venison, wild rice flavored with maple sugar, smoked trout, and a delicious stewed meat served in laced vessels molded out of white birch bark.

As much as Pierre enjoyed the food, he couldn't help admiring Mukwa's oldest daughter, Kennewah, who passed dishes to the guests. Pierre expected the whole family to be dressed in gaudy clothing like their father, but Kennewah wore a simple white doeskin dress. Her eyes were deep brown and soft.

Kennewah's gentle and quiet manner reminded Pierre of Celeste. It had been six weeks since he'd talked to a person his own age. There were a hundred questions he wanted to ask, but the boldest thing he brought himself to offer was a smile.

A baby, who was about the same age as Pierre's little

sister Claire, sat across from him during the meal. Whenever Pierre winked at the child, he grinned broadly.

"Kewatin has found a friend," Mukwa commented, proud that his guest paid attention to his young son.

Charbonneau and Mukwa spent the evening talking about old times. La Londe's name came up more than once. It was clear he'd been a good friend to them both. Pierre listened quietly, but when Mukwa called La Londe Snake Bite, Pierre asked why.

Charbonneau grinned. "He was deathly afraid of snakes. It's funny, too, 'cause none of us ever knew it until we went on a scouting trip down the Red River one spring. Mukwa was our guide. We were checking out the trading possibilities, and things were going along until we camped on a feeder stream of the Red one night. It was a low, boggy area, but we couldn't afford to be choosy since it was getting dark. We'd no sooner pitched our tent and crawled under our blankets when La Londe let out a yelp and jumped up. A snake had tried to crawl up his leggings. We all laughed. It was just a harmless water snake, but La Londe was so riled up he nearly pulled the tent down. To calm him we lit a tallow candle and searched the bedding. Altogether we found three or four of the little rascals."

Pierre shuddered at the thought.

"We threw the snakes out the door, tied the flap down tight, and got La Londe settled in. Everything would have been fine if Mukwa here hadn't played the funny man and given La Londe's big toe a hard pinch. Poor fellow jumped up again, yelping, 'I'm bit. I'm snakebit.'

" 'There's nothing to worry about, La Londe,' Mukwa said. 'Them's just water snakes, livin' in those old graves down by the river.' "

"After that comment"—Charbonneau shook his head and grinned—"he was too spooked to even think about sleeping. Poor fellow sat up the rest of the night staring at the tent flap with his blanket wrapped around him, muttering, 'Snakes in graves.' "

"He caught up on his sleep the next day," Mukwa added.

"La Londe could take a passable nap in the saddle," Charbonneau said, chuckling. "He only fell off his horse twice all day."

"But that's what ended up saving our skins at the end of it all," Mukwa said.

Charbonneau nodded. He and Mukwa sat in silence a moment, pondering something that had happened long ago, but the talking was done.

A short while later Charbonneau and Pierre thanked Mukwa for his hospitality. Mukwa gave Charbonneau a hug, and Pierre bowed politely to both the chief and his family. On the way back to the fort, Pierre's curiosity got the best of him. "What did Mukwa mean by La Londe saving your skins?" he asked.

Charbonneau didn't answer right away. He began with

a sigh. "The next day we were coming up on a ridge when La Londe, who'd been snoring for at least a mile, tumbled off his horse. Mukwa and I dismounted to help him, when we heard some commotion just ahead. We tethered our horses and belly-crawled up a hill. Below us was a Sioux war party, marching south. A string of ponies stretched around the ridge and clear out of sight. The faces of the warriors were splattered with grime and blood. Scalp poles were slung over their shoulders. A long, blond cascade of hair dangled from one pole, and we were close enough to see a pearl comb still tucked in place. It turned your stomach."

He took a deep breath. "But the worst was the three little golden locks of hair on the next pole. Before we knew it, La Londe cocked his North West gun and drew a bead on a Sioux. It would have been suicide, but I thought he was going to fire.

"After the last warrior passed, La Londe still lay there, his gun cocked, sighting on the horizon. There were tears running down his cheeks."

Pierre was still thinking of La Londe when Charbonneau changed the subject. Charbonneau whispered, "Look," and pointed toward the waning moon. Below its slender arc, star-flecked Superior stretched farther than Pierre could see. At that moment as they stood alone in the silvery dark above the fort, Pierre remembered that he was halfway home.

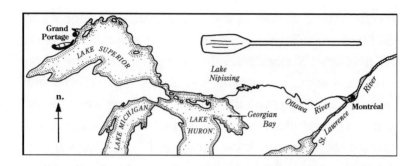

CHAPTER 19

◆

Rendezvous

OVER BREAKFAST THE next morning, Charbonneau asked, "So what'd you think of that dog at Mukwa's?"

Pierre recalled the critter that guarded Mukwa's wigwam. It reminded him of his own dog, Pepper. "He was friendly enough."

Charbonneau laughed. "I don't mean the one you were petting," he said, "I'm talking about the one you ate."

"Ate?"

"What did you think was in that stew you were chucking down so fast?"

Remembering the scrawny mutts he'd seen around

the Indian camp, Pierre fought the nausea back. "Dog, eh?"

Charbonneau nodded. "I know it's hard to get used to, but out here everything is tied to survival. You live off what the land offers: hazelnuts, cattail root, beaver—it all fills the gut. Dog to the Indians can mean pulling a sled, carrying a pack, or meat on the table."

Pierre was still trying to decide if he thought it was right to eat dog—wilderness or not—after Charbonneau had excused himself and headed for the fur-pressing room.

Later that morning Pierre went for a hike on the hill behind the fort. Skirting the edge of the Indian village, he followed a deer trail that ran parallel to the lake. A short while later he came to a clearing that offered a spectacular view of Superior. Below him a dozen canoes were rounding Hat Point and racing for the fort.

He was staring at the brigade pulling for the fort when a voice startled him. "You like Gitchegammi?"

He turned to find the pretty girl, Kennewah, holding a birch bark basket in her hand and smiling broadly. Pierre felt himself blush.

"You like Gitchegammi?" She repeated in faltering French. For a moment he thought she was referring to the blueberries in her basket, but when he looked down, she shook her head and pointed toward the lake. Pierre nodded, understanding that Kennewah was using the Ojibwa word for Lake Superior.

"Yes, I do," he said.

Kennewah, still smiling, asked, "You like Kennewah?"

Such directness shocked Pierre. He wasn't sure what to say.

"You like Kennewah?" she repeated.

"Yes," he said, looking into her dark brown eyes.

When the canoe race below concluded, Kennewah motioned toward a berry patch, inviting Pierre to help with the picking. They turned to walk up the ridge. He thought of offering his hand, but before he could make up his mind, she gave his hand a friendly squeeze and led him to the place where the blueberry bushes were thickest.

Kennewah knelt and, working with both hands at once, began to fill her basket. Rolling her fingers through the low bushes, she filled each palm in a single, graceful motion and dropped the berries into her basket.

Pierre often picked berries with his mother and sister back in Lachine. They always teased him about being a better eater than a picker. When he was little, Mother sometimes threatened to limit him to a single piece of blueberry pie if he didn't fill his bucket more and his face less.

Today Pierre tried to pick as fast as Kennewah, but he ended up with only a handful of leaves. She giggled in a gentle way that made Pierre chuckle at himself. He smiled when she leaned close to him and touched his hair, saying the French word for *white, blanc.* He shook his head and tried to explain *blond* to her, but she only laughed and pushed a huge berry between his lips. He chewed it slowly, savoring the sun-warmed sweetness.

After they were through picking berries, they walked back to the village together. Though their talk was limited to simple French phrases, Pierre was surprised at how much they could say with only a gesture or smile.

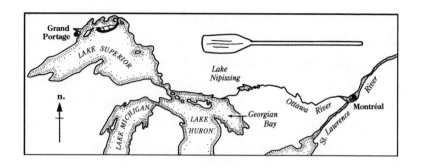

CHAPTER 20

Rubbaboo

ON THE MORNING of their departure all five canoes were loaded by three A.M. Lake Superior lay still and silver gray. Pierre knew it was important to start early and paddle hard on the big lake in midsummer, because violent winds often made travel impossible by early afternoon.

As the brigade pushed off from the pier, each *voyageur* crossed himself and whispered a prayer before he took up his paddle. La Petite, choosing not to disturb the mist-quiet morning with a song, whistled a soft tune instead.

Commander McKay and Emile and the other *hivernants* had gone north the day before. New hands were hired on to replace those that wouldn't be returning. The previous morning, Emile had shaken Pierre's hand before he started up the famous portage and said, "Make sure you don't beat up Belly Boy too often." Belly Boy was a nickname Emile had used for Beloît since the day Pierre punched the bowman in the stomach.

"I promise," Pierre said, laughing. "And you keep your powder dry."

"Until next year?" Emile grinned, turning up the trail.

"We'll see," Pierre called after him.

After McKay checked one last bill of lading, he took Pierre aside and said, "You listen to Charbonneau and La Petite on the way back to Montréal, lad. If you learn as much going home as you did on our outward trip, you'll be wintering with us soon."

Then McKay reached in his pack and pulled out a leather-bound book. "I thought I'd loan you a bit of reading material to keep you occupied on the way home."

Pierre's eyes widened as he opened the volume to the longest title he'd ever seen: *The Journals and Letters of Pierre Gaultier de Varennes de La Vérendrye and His Sons.* Pierre had always wanted to read about La Vérendrye, the most famous of all French Canadian explorers.

"Thank you, sir," was all Pierre had a chance to say before McKay waved one last time to the crewmen he was leaving behind and started up the Grand Portage trail.

That same afternoon Mukwa stopped by their camp to say goodbye. The chief embraced Charbonneau and wished him luck on his "many-days paddle." Then he turned and pumped Pierre's arm hard, calling him "my friend's friend" and saying, "You must visit us again soon. Kennewah wishes you a safe journey, too. Perhaps you will come next season?"

"Tell her to look for me next June," Pierre replied.

Though Pierre would miss this place, he was glad to be heading back to Lachine. When he thought of Kennewah and her straight-parted hair and shy smile, he longed for the gentler pleasures of home. Tired of smoke and grease and unwashed men, he was looking forward to simple things such as sitting at a clean table and eating a meal of his mother's roast chicken and blueberry pie, soaking in a tub of hot water, and sleeping on the soft ticking of his old bed.

As the painted prows swung east, Pierre saw the dark eyes of Kennewah and her quiet lodge up on the hill. He would return to Grand Portage. His first journey was made out of duty to his family, but next time he would voyage here on his own account. He'd been thinking a lot about what Mr. McKay had said about tending to his studies. If he could use his schooling to secure a place as an officer of the company someday, that would give him the best of both worlds. He could learn and profit and adventure all at once.

One by one the paddlers began their steady dip and pull.

"So what do you think of our new boat, Pierre?" Charbonneau asked proudly.

"It looks narrower than our old one."

"You've got a good eye for canoes. It's speed we want, and just like the clipper ships back East, trimmer is faster."

"She's a beauty," Pierre agreed. As he studied the clean, new ash of the gunwales, he remembered his father telling him how important it was to "pull his own weight." On the route home he would make up for any weakness he'd shown earlier.

I'll paddle as I've never paddled before, he promised himself. Pierre strained with his arms and shoulders, forgetting that the legs and back are the key. He pulled hard and fast, forgetting that pace is everything to the canoeman. Soon he was forced to catch his breath, and before they cleared the harbor, his muscles ached.

Suddenly he was angry with himself. How had he forgotten La Londe and Charbonneau's advice so soon? When he finally caught the old rhythm, he smiled. Thinking back to his first days on the Ottawa, Pierre soon forgot his paddle altogether and "cheated" his work by dreaming.

Time passed in a blur. The paddling and pipe stops fell into their familiar pattern as the sun tracked its way across the sky. A western breeze came up by midmorning and helped push them on.

Anxious to take advantage of the conditions, La Petite and Charbonneau kept the rest stops short. "Work your blades, boys," one or the other would sing out, "when the Old Lady of the Wind smiles, it is a sin not to fly." Scorning the pleasant weather as he scorned all things, Beloît was silent.

By early evening they'd traveled nearly seventy miles. Then Charbonneau steered his boat alongside La Petite's and called out, "That's Nipigon Point just ahead. Should we call it a day?" Pierre's heart thrilled at the prospect of rest.

"Fine with me, Charbonneau," La Petite replied, sculling his oar with practiced ease.

"Though these fellows haven't pushed the issue," Charbonneau said, motioning with his paddle toward his crewmen, "I know they're itching to test the speed of their boat." Pierre turned angrily. He couldn't believe the man would suggest a race after they'd paddled for fourteen hours.

"I thought, maybe, you got beatings enough on our first trip to last you all the way back home?" La Petite teased.

"But this is a new canoe."

"Your men are the same, Charbonneau. Don't kid yourself. The canoe doesn't paddle itself." Then, turning to his crew, La Petite continued, "What you say, fellows? Shall we give these amateurs a lesson?"

A moment later all five canoes were racing for Nipigon Point.

Pierre paddled without enthusiasm. He thought, Why not just save our strength for carrying the firewood and for taking the teasing that is sure to follow?

It wasn't until they were halfway to shore that Pierre finally became excited about the race. La Petite's canoe was just off their port bow and opening up a half-length lead. Beloît turned to check the progress of the other three craft. Pierre assumed that the rear canoes were getting ready to pass them, as they usually did in the middle of a race, but Beloît grinned and yelled, "Pull, ladies, pull. We bury them."

Pierre turned, and to his astonishment saw that their canoe was two lengths ahead of the next one. In his moment of inattention, he splashed the man ahead of him and nearly dropped his paddle in the lake. "Paddle, La Page," Charbonneau said, and cursed.

Pierre whirled his blade. Here was their chance to avenge six long weeks of losing. As La Petite's canoe pulled ahead by a full length, the big man turned and teased them, doffing his cap and waving goodbye as if he were about to board a fancy carriage.

"Let's learn them not to celebrate so soon," Charbonneau called.

Beloît yelled, "Yes! Yes!" as the men pursed their lips and pulled for all they were worth.

Charbonneau's canoe closed to a half a length and was still gaining when La Petite glanced back, expecting to find a safe distance. Shocked, he took a big, sweeping stroke with his steersman's paddle and yelled, "Press hard, fellows!"

Pierre saw that two of La Petite's crew were startled by the sudden shout and missed their strokes. La Petite yelled again, but Charbonneau's men pulled all the faster.

Though La Petite won by a paddle length, Pierre was elated to see the final canoe in the brigade still a hundred yards offshore.

"So what do you think of the new boat now, Pierre?" Charbonneau said with a smile as he stepped into the water and turned their craft parallel to the beach so that the middlemen could unload.

"It's hard to believe it can be that much faster."

"It is not all the canoe. When you paddle a bad boat it builds big muscles." Charbonneau squeezed Pierre's biceps and made his eyes go wide. "Now we are ready for the races."

Charbonneau's crew had their canoe unloaded before the last craft arrived. Standing with his arms crossed, Charbonneau claimed bragging rights. He waited until the last canoe pulled in, and then he waited still longer. When the men were convinced he wasn't going to speak at all, he yawned, like a man who had been waiting too long in the sun. "Could you tell me, gentlemen," he asked, "why soup tastes sweeter when it is warmed by another man's wood?" Laughter echoed up and down the beach.

That evening Pierre was surprised when Bellegarde made a delicious concoction called rubbaboo for supper. Made from pemmican and flour and a bit of sugar, it was rich in flavor compared to their ordinary ration of salt pork and corn. When Pierre noticed that La Petite had taken a place at the head of the line, he teased him. "Not only is our famous steersman fast on the water," Pierre said, "but he is quick to get at the cooking pot." The crewmen laughed.

"Hush up and eat, La Page," La Petite countered.

"Forgive me, sir," Pierre said, "but I am only a poor student, learning how to paddle my canoe."

As Bellegarde ladled up generous portions of his specialty, the men were quick to show their praise. "You are an *artiste* with a cooking pot, *monsieur,*" Charbonneau said as he watched the greasy little man load his plate, "and your intelligence is surpassed only by the quality of the company you keep."

"Pouring it on a bit thick, aren't you, Charbonneau?" La Petite called out from across the fire.

"Talent needs praise to flourish."

"Why don't you tell the truth," La Petite insisted, "and admit that you're just happy to see someone else gather the wood for once?" Several of the company seconded the comment. "Besides, Charbonneau," La Petite continued, "you forget I wintered with you up on the Red River and—"

"I defy you to—"

"And," La Petite continued, "I got plenty sick of your whining about the rancid buffalo fat and rotten serviceberries that were bagged in the name of pemmican."

"But this," Charbonneau insisted, "is finer and more delicate fare. Anyone can tell."

La Petite caught Bellegarde's attention, asking, "Where was this pemmican made?"

There was a pause while Bellegarde thought. "I believe McKay said it came from Pembina." The men, knowing that Pembina was a post on the Red River, instantly burst into laughter.

Pierre stared at his plate. The black fibers that he'd assumed were strands of dried buffalo meat looked suspiciously like hair. He leaned in La Petite's direction and whispered, "Is there ever hair in pemmican?"

"Is there water in a lake?"

Pierre frowned. "What sort of hair would it be?"

La Petite was still catching his breath from his hard laugh. "It depends. It might be buffalo, coyote, prairie dog, human—who knows? Sometimes it might be a mix of several kinds of critters."

Pierre looked down at his plate again. He was hungry for something simple like boiled corn.

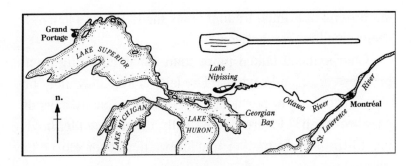

CHAPTER 21

Homeward Bound

THE GOOD WEATHER held for their entire traverse of Lake Superior. "Let's push, men," Charbonneau or La Petite urged each morning as they noted the clarity of the sky. Remembering the near disaster on Michipicoten Bay, Pierre understood their anxiety on the big lake. Charbonneau reminded them of their good fortune each day, saying, "You must say the right prayers, fellows."

Pierre's muscles adjusted quickly to the familiar work of paddling. He enjoyed the portage-free travel and pulled from pipe stop to pipe stop like a veteran. When time allowed in the evening, Pierre read La Vérendrye's book. The distances the famous explorer traveled in establishing dozens of French trading posts made Pierre's journey seem small by comparison.

Charbonneau talked more than usual, admiring their progress often and saying, "The lake is a holiday, no?" or "We forget how to portage, maybe, with so many days of easy work, eh?" Pierre agreed with a nod or smile, holding to the steady motion that drew them ever closer to home.

The brigade passed through Sault Sainte Marie in a festive mood. Each clear, bright day the *chansons* of the canoemen echoed up the rocky shore of Huron. It wasn't until the brigade neared the French River that a gloomy silence descended.

Long before they reached the river mouth, the canoemen saw La Londe's red marker high up on the hill. They shipped their oars for a moment and floated across the still water. Doffing their caps and bowing their heads, the men crossed themselves and offered silent prayers.

Pierre remembered the broken blade La Petite had retrieved that afternoon. As he recalled the searching faces and the darkening water, the old emptiness rose up inside him. No matter how hard or how often he thought of that day, there was no way he could make sense out of it.

Halfway up the French River, the brigade took a pipe stop. Pierre sat at the base of a tall pine and drew out the knife La Londe had given him.

He was whittling a stick when Charbonneau sat down next to him, saying, "I'll bet it has beautiful balance."

Charbonneau hefted the knife by its bone handle and nodded. "Just like every one he ever made." He handed it back to Pierre and leaned against the pine trunk, taking a deep pull on his pipe.

"I know it's hard," he continued. "Every single one of us misses him. But it's a part of what we accept on the trail. It can happen to anyone—me and you included—at any minute."

Pierre nodded, grateful to the steersman for offering comfort. Then Charbonneau asked, "Did your father ever tell you the Tale of the Lost Child?"

Pierre shook his head.

"It's an old Indian legend. Everyone who's paddled the French has heard it. According to the story, an Ojibwa family was camped right here in this grove. A boy who was playing by the river slipped off that ledge"— Charbonneau pointed toward the river as he spoke—"and he vanished without a sound. The family searched the bank and paddled downriver, calling his name, but there was no sign of him."

Pierre looked from Charbonneau to the river. "Then, just when they were ready to give up, they heard the boy's voice coming from under the ground. They dug as fast as they could, scraping a hole with a hatchet blade. For a while the crying was so loud it seemed as if they could reach down and touch the boy's hand. They kept digging, but the voice drifted off. It moved away from the river, staying deep underground. When they finally gave up, the cries were coming from beneath that cliff back there, and the voice was growing fainter by the moment."

Charbonneau stared at the river for a long time after the story was done. Pierre finally broke the silence, asking, "Do you believe that could really happen?"

With his eyes still fixed on the river, Charbonneau replied slowly, "You mean, is it true?"

Pierre nodded.

"All I can say for sure is that I heard the story told by lots and lots of fellows. That gives it a sort of truth, I guess. The more I learn about these rivers, the more I realize there's hundreds of things we'll never understand. There's too many moods, too many feelings that shift with the seasons. All we can ever know for sure is the changes."

At that moment La Petite interrupted, asking, "Time to voyage?" Charbonneau rose and tapped his pipe against the tree trunk.

The French River was in a quiet, low-water mood, totally unlike the bright roaring that had washed La Londe and the lost child of the legend to their graves. After they started paddling again, Pierre thought about the wild river, and he listened for that little Ojibwa boy's cries.

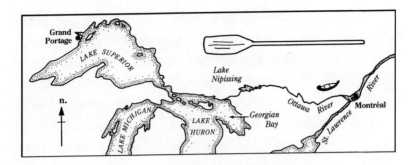

CHAPTER 22

◆

The Last Portage

THE DAYS MELDED together, and once they reached the Ottawa, home seemed within reach. Though Lachine was still three hundred miles distant, Pierre was confident their trip would be over soon.

Their first morning on the Ottawa, Pierre spoke with Charbonneau during breakfast. "It's just a downstream coast from here, eh?"

"Well," Charbonneau said, glancing at the sluggish river, "that depends."

"On what? Shouldn't we go twice as fast downstream?"

"We should, but the current may be weaker than you remember."

True to Charbonneau's word, the country got progressively drier. The river was a mere trickle in places, and their progress was as slow as their upstream travel had been in the spring. Many of the rapids were unsafe to run, and short stretches they'd tracked or paddled *demi-chargé* in May were now portages.

Pierre suddenly felt as if he'd never get home. The miles seemed like years. Images of Lachine grew hazy, and the harder he tried to fix the pictures in his mind, the faster they slipped away. Sometimes in the middle of a paddle stroke, a face would flash before him. With the suddenness of a scarf pulled from a magician's sleeve, his mother or father or Celeste would appear. Yet as quickly as the shapes become whole, they faded.

The vanishing scared Pierre. There was no calling the faces back once they were gone. It reminded him too much of the way he felt about La Londe.

As they worked their way downriver, Pierre thought more and more about his father. He replayed the wood-chopping accident in his mind and worried about the summer of pain that Father must have suffered. He feared that the jumbled images in his head meant something bad was to come. To forget his worries, he tried reading La Vérendrye's journal during the long summer evenings, but the explorer's stories about his search for a western passage to the sea and the death of his son on Massacre Island made Pierre more homesick than ever.

Charbonneau noticed his impatience one evening as

they sat before the fire. "If you want a thing too badly it never comes," he said.

"It shows that much?"

"To survive," Charbonneau continued, "you must look on the journey the same as your paddling."

"But the time goes so slowly."

"That is the sweetness of the traveling life. Time is frozen by the journey. While most men worry away their lives, counting coins and filling ledgers, we *voyageurs* live with the magic of the open water." Charbonneau looked from the river to the distant hills as he talked. "We travel as the sun and wind allow. All the places we've been are with us every moment of our lives."

Just then Michel Larocque walked by the campfire. Pierre teased him. "So how are the legs holding up, old fellow?"

"Old fellow?" Larocque repeated, stopping to glare at Pierre.

"That's right." Pierre grinned. "I've heard that jumpers age real fast if they don't get their practice."

"We shall see." Larocque immediately turned to gather wood.

When the fire was roaring, Larocque approached Pierre. "After you, *monsieur*," he said, gesturing toward the dancing flames.

Pierre stood and stretched his legs. Knowing it was best not to hesitate, he trotted to the far end of the camp. Then he turned back toward the fire, sprinting hard. He leaped. Fearing for a moment that he'd jumped too soon, Pierre wheeled his arms and extended his feet straight out. The flames singed his calves, but he landed clear of the embers and rolled immediately back to his feet.

The crewmen cheered. Larocque laughed and clapped him on the shoulder. "A fine leap, Pierre. I see our hard portaging has toughened your legs as well as your back."

As Larocque and a dozen other men jumped the fire, Pierre thought back to the night when La Londe and Beloît had rolled in the ashes and tried to beat each other senseless. Though it was only a month or so ago, it seemed as if a lifetime had passed.

Time reeled backward as the brigade shot the turbulent Roche Capitaine and made the long carries at Des Joachims and the Grand Calumet. Though it did little to quiet Pierre's mind, they drew ever closer to home, leaving Chats Falls, Deschenes, and the Chaudières behind.

On the Long Sault, just two days shy of home, they met one of the few brigades still heading north. The outfit was bound for Mackinac and the leader of the group stopped to ask Charbonneau about the water level on the upper reaches of the river. Pierre shouldered his parcels, anxious to complete what promised to be the final carry of the trip.

When Pierre arrived on the shore of Two Mountain Lake, the last group in a northbound brigade was just starting out. Two grinning men knelt before an open pack. One fellow said, "This should fix young Nolin," while the second man stuffed something into the blankets at the top of the pack. He chuckled as he pulled the straps down tight.

Pierre knew what they were planning. He tossed down his parcels and hurried back up the trail. He would find the boy and warn him about the trick.

When Pierre finally met a timid young *voyageur* he asked, "Are you Nolin?"

The boy, startled that a stranger would know his name, nodded.

Pierre was about to say "It might be wise to check your next pack," but he stopped. As he studied the determination in the boy's eyes, Pierre suddenly saw himself on his own first portage. In that instant he realized it would be wrong to take the thing from this boy that was his right to earn. So instead of warning him, Pierre nodded curtly, just as he knew the old-timers would, and said, "Have a good journey."

Then Pierre was off to complete his final carry.

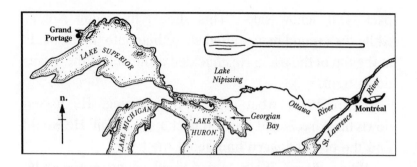

CHAPTER 23

The Woodpile

THE BRIGADE ARRIVED in Lachine on a quiet August evening. Once the pelts were delivered to the company warehouse, Pierre shouldered his pack and headed for home.

Just before he turned onto the road that led to his cabin, he approached Dr. Guilliard's house. Pierre closed his eyes and shivered as he recalled the mad dash he'd made last spring.

"La Page! Pierre La Page!" Guilliard called out.

Pierre looked up, surprised to see the doctor, his wife, and Celeste all sitting on the front porch.

"Good evening, Doctor," Pierre said, touching his cap.

"Is McKay's brigade back already?" Guilliard asked.

158

"We just got in this evening, sir." Pierre paused at Guilliard's front gate.

"Did you have a good trip?" the doctor asked.

"Yes . . ." Pierre paused, thinking about how impossible it would be to reduce the last three months of his life to a single answer. For now he would leave it simple. "Yes," he repeated. "We had a fine trip."

"You must stop by sometime," Mrs. Guilliard interjected, "and tell us about your travels."

"I'd like that," Pierre said, smiling at Celeste. "Hello, Celeste," he said.

Celeste blushed and lowered her eyes before she spoke. He remembered her as bold and self-confident, yet today she looked pale and shy. Since Celeste's reply was impossible to hear, Pierre simply smiled. "Nice seeing you folks," he said, "but I really have to get home."

"Of course," Dr. Guilliard said, "but do stop by again."

"Thank you, sir. I will."

Pierre heard the ax from a long way off. Even before he got within sight of the cabin, the ringing of the steel told him his father was splitting oak. As he walked up the trail, he recalled the day last spring when he had sprinted down this same path.

He balked at the thought that it had happened just last May. He shook his head and wondered how time could play such tricks. It seemed as if half his life had passed since that day. Just then he heard a bark, and his dog,

Pepper, ran out of the brush. Pierre knelt and greeted his old friend. The whole time he petted the dog, he could still hear the steady ringing of Father's ax.

At the edge of the clearing Pierre laid down his pack. His moccasins were silent as he and Pepper crept toward the cabin to surprise his father. They were screened by a tall pine until they were nearly to the woodshed, but as soon as Pierre tiptoed around the corner of the cabin, his father looked up.

Reacting to some small movement, or sensing his presence out of instinct, as woodsmen often do, Father looked over his shoulder. The ax was suspended high over his head. In a single motion he released the blade and pivoted toward his son. Pierre sucked in his breath and closed his eyes tight. He could see the ax slashing into his father's leg.

Instead he heard the solid thunk of wood, and he looked up again. By then, Father was halfway to him. Before Father had a chance to shout, Pierre put his finger to his lips and shook his head, signaling to keep his arrival a secret. Teary-eyed, Father crushed him in a long, silent hug.

"Let me have a look at you," Father whispered, stepping back to hold him at arm's length. As they stood eye to eye, Pierre was surprised to see he was nearly as tall as his father.

They shook hands, and Father raised his eyebrows when he felt the new strength in Pierre's grip. He grinned like a man who had found a son long given up for dead. Pierre was worried, though, by the strange way his father shook his head from side to side.

"Is something wrong?" Pierre asked, but his father just stared. "I said, 'Is there something wrong?'"

Father chuckled, saying, "Not something, but everything."

"What do you mean?" Pierre asked. "Is Mother all right?"

"No. No. Nothing like that."

"What do you mean, then?"

"Is it not wrong to send a boy off and have him never come back?"

"I'm back."

"But you're not the same." Father studied the confusion in his son's face. He concluded finally by saying, "No. Somewhere along the trail you buried my boy and resurrected a man in his place."

Father was laughing now and giving his son a second hug. Pierre had trouble believing he'd changed that much. From boy to man, he thought, in a single summer? He looked over his shoulder toward the house to see if anyone had heard the commotion.

As Father stepped back, Pierre couldn't help staring at the stub of his father's thumb, stretched tight as it was with skin that looked smoother and shinier than the rest of his hand.

Father saw him staring at the injured thumb and suddenly lifted it level with his son's eyes. "You have nothing to worry about where this little stump is concerned," he said. "It healed quick and never slowed me down even half a lick. Feel it." He paused, tapping the stub on Pierre's shoulder. "It works just as good as a regular thumb, and it's tough as a chunk of seasoned cordwood." Still grinning, Father thumped his scarred appendage twice against the front of his own thigh to prove his point.

"Why don't you take a rest?" Pierre asked, nodding in the direction of the woodpile, "and let me finish up the splitting?"

Father frowned. "This is no time to chop wood. We've got some serious celebrating to do."

"Once you step inside the house," Pierre said, "I suspect it won't take Mother long to figure out the wood isn't splitting itself." Father nodded then, agreeing it would be a fine joke.

He studied his son's weather-toughened face while Pierre walked to the wood block and pulled the ax free with one hand. It felt good to balance the familiar hickory handle in his hands. The dark, oiled grain was smooth against his callused palms. As he hefted the ax, Pierre was surprised that it felt no heavier than a paddle blade.

He set a block of wood in place and swung. With the flat crack of a branch snapping off in midwinter cold, the blade sheared the oak block in two. The perfect halves fell onto the packed earth with a thud and rocked for an instant before they were still. Pierre smiled when he saw how deeply the ax head was buried in the chopping block. Then, with a grin that bettered his son's, Father hurried off toward the cabin.

About the Author

William Durbin is a Minneapolis-born teacher and writer who has lived in the lake country of northeastern Minnesota for the past twenty years. A graduate of the Bread Loaf School of English, he teaches English at a small, rural high school and composition at a community college. He has published a variety of poetry and prose in literary and professional journals, and he has written a biography of golfer Tiger Woods which will be released later this year. *The Broken Blade* is his first novel.